large animals in everyday life

large animals

Winner of the Flannery O'Connor Award for Short Fiction

In everyday life

Stories by Wendy Brenner

The University of Georgia Press • Athens & London

Published by the University of Georgia Press
Athens, Georgia 30602
© 1996 by Wendy Brenner
All rights reserved
Designed by Erin Kirk New
Set in 10.5 on 14 Berkeley Old Style Medium
by Books International
Printed and bound by Maple-Vail Book Manufacturing Group
The paper in this book meets the guidelines for permanence
and durability of the Committee on Production Guidelines
for Book Longevity of the Council on Library Resources.

Printed in the United States of America

00 99 98 97 96 C 5 4 3 2 1

Library of Congress Cataloging in Publication Data

Brenner, Wendy.
    Large animals in everyday life : stories / by Wendy
Brenner.
        p.   cm.
    ISBN 0-8203-1794-2 (alk. paper)
    1. Manners and customs—Fiction.   I. Title.
PS3552.R3863L37   1996
813'.54—dc20   95-21692

British Library Cataloging in Publication Data available

Thanks to the editors of the following publications where
some of these stories first appeared: *Beloit Fiction Journal*:
"Easy"; *Mississippi Review*: "I Am the Bear"; *New Delta
Review*: "The Round Bar"; *New England Review*: "A Little
Something"; *Ploughshares*: "The Oysters"; *Puerto del Sol*:
"Success Story"; *Southern Exposure*: "Undisclosed Location";
Yemassee: "Guest Speaker."

For their faith and support, thanks also to the Henfield
Foundation, the AWP Intro Journals Project, and Charles
East, and to Dina Ben-lev, Tasha Malinchoc, and Jamie
Arthur.

To Lisa Wright, Jim Shea,

and the memory of

my grandmothers

We all growl like bears,

like doves we moan without ceasing.

We look for right, but it is not there . . .

   Isaiah 59:11

Fish, if not exactly leading rich, emotional lives,

have developed some very peculiar characteristics.

   Joy Williams, *The Florida Keys: A History and Guide*

contents

large animals in everyday life

shop, then goes outside and drinks beer in the sun, and the dogs bite the lawnmower. They live in the woods, no mailbox, no anything, nothing but fine green land all around, bashful buffalo herd on the prairie bordering. I almost lived out there with that man and those dogs, but the man was skinny and sneaky, no chest on him, and he tried to write certain things into the lease, which wasn't after all much of a surprise or disappointment because you don't get men and dogs and land together like that for free.

Though I was expected to develop into a successful practicing artist (I was admitted into my grammar school's Accelerated Program for the Specially Gifted in the Audio, Visual, and Kinetic Arts based on my performance on a test requiring me to create a picture of my own imagining around an empty bean shape which suggested to me the torso of a sad, keening dog, which I drew), instead I spend my time at the Round Bar, where there are both animals and men and you can either rotate or sit your chair on the part of the floor that doesn't move. Sometimes there I even see the skinny sneaky man and we raise hands, no hard feelings, and I pet Red and Blue, who lie flat beside the seam in the linoleum, trying to bite the floor as it goes by.

But the main reason I go is to see the singer, a dwarfish Kentucky native who, though he once toured seven Southern states in a band opening for Conway Twitty, now plays alone and only for tips—"The Lord will take care of me," he says—and whose business card reads NOT JUST A GENTLEMAN BUT A GENTLEMAN, though sitting with his heavy shoulders hunched around his twelve-string he does not look gentle or for that matter short. He always plays the same songs, sometimes twice in one night: "Make the World Go Away," "From a Jack to a King," "Where Am I Gonna Live When I Get Home?" but no one complains; patrons of the Round Bar, deep in their stubborn Southern drunks, cannot resist the singer for long. They approach him shyly all night, like third-graders walking to the front of the class, to put dollars in his plastic pitcher and touch his mikestand or his arm, or the women dance right in front of him, shaking their hips and looking into his dangerous eyes, or the men try to shake his hand that's on the guitar and after a while give up and go sit back down, looking embarrassed but happy, as happy as you could imagine them ever looking. And I sit in my booth on the wall and wait, happy to wait, because between sets the singer will come over and say, "Hello, young lady," and something very big will seem to be happening.

Interestingly, my father came from a long line of musicians, "players, primarily, of stringed instruments"—this is verbatim from a Xerox of a family history he researched and wrote years ago but forgot about and only found in his papers last year and sent me with my monthly check. His grandfather's father, it was rumored, had requested that his violin be buried with him when he died. "How can I be an adult and not have known this?" I wrote to my father, and he wrote back, "We wanted to assure you, as always, that we support you in your independent artistic pursuits." I was so excited about this evidence of kismet that I went immediately to the Round Bar and asked the singer if he played violin, and he smiled faintly as though remembering far back and said, "Used to could, used to could."

But the Xerox also revealed that my father's second cousin Larry was an idiot savant: *Larry's family had no inkling of his hidden talents but saw only that he lacked the most basic of skills for coping with the everyday world. Then one day when he was ten years of age he was riding with his mother Fannie on a Chicago streetcar and began emitting strange utterances. 'A . . . G . . . B flat,' Larry would exclaim, and so on, each time the car stopped. Finally Fannie realized he was declaring the exact key in which the brakes had squealed. Larry, though severely retarded, had perfect pitch.* But Larry was never able to learn how to tie his own shoelaces or even lift a fork to his own mouth, the Xerox said, and he died under uninvestigated circumstances at the age of thirty-three in a state institution. "Did you send me this information to imply that I have not striven hard enough to succeed in the arts or that I am somehow doomed?" I wrote my father from my booth at the Round Bar, and my father wrote back, "In answer to your question, certainly not. Your mother and I believe you are doing everything within your power to forge your own way in these difficult times."

Everyone in the arts hated me anyway. What happened was that there was so much talk at us from teachers in the program about boyfriends and prettiness not mattering that by sixth grade I knew I would rather die than not have both. The arts were easy, fuck it. I planned to impress everyone and teach them something new by showing them some hot sex. In photo lab that year I did a series of me in cutoffs letting a garter snake I'd caught wind around my neck and head down toward my unsnapped fly, and then in a talent show I performed a gypsy dance to "Magic Man," also wearing the snake and cutoffs but with strips of red velvet tied on my wrists and ankles, and afterward when Dr. Bearwald, the emcee and also incidentally the one who had administered the empty bean test, said, "It will be difficult for anyone to top that but now let's move on," I did not cry, even though the snake had bitten me twice during my dance and it really hurt. And later, when he had me in to his office to ask me my career goals and I told him I wanted to become a model and he said casually, "You can't, you're not pretty enough," his face looking like it was made out of wax, pink wax under black wax hair, I knew that though I was talking to a wax man now, down the road, in the invisible room of my future, real men who would have loved the snake and the velvet were waiting. I imagined them leaning casually against a long bar, big men made of skin and dirt, smoking and scuffing the toes of their boots on the cement floor. And I found these men, finally, at the Round Bar, and it was a relief.

For one winter after my formal training in the arts was complete I had tried to make a go of it in San Diego with an art librarian who spoke in a controlled whisper even outside the library, who never got angry but was secretly always angry, breezing around in seersucker suits and straw boaters and refusing to raise his voice. He himself was not an artist but had devoted his life to the preserving and cataloguing of art and claimed to be real happy about that, very satisfied; he also shopped for me at Victoria's Secret and said I was the second most intelligent woman he ever met (the first was Hannah Arendt) and claimed to be able to feel it in his own nipple when he touched mine. He was much older than me, however, and over me in bed his eye bags hung down and I was beside myself trying not to notice them or acknowledge that they mattered. The real problem, finally, wasn't his eye bags or even him, that much, but the city, which seemed to me unnatural for no good reason I could pinpoint except that the buildings, like any buildings but for some reason these really bothered me, lacked the integrity of natural creation. Buildings were false, I was just realizing at twenty-two (duh). Yes, we needed them, but we didn't need so *many* of them, or such big ones. "I don't like it here," I said often, and the librarian would drape himself over me, saying, "Oh, *baby*," trying to be some kind of spiritual blanket but at the same time getting, as he called it, *aroused* because he thought I looked like an aerobics teacher, which to him was a perversion: lowly physicality combined with bouncing commercialism, the dirty opposite of art.

So I drank, which made me feel that someone, I didn't know who, who could make me feel better about something, I didn't know what, was in the room with me or at least reachable by phone. Or, to get out of the house, I visited the Pai Gow Indian Reservation casino. There people didn't talk to each other much, but everyone was in a wonderful mood, solid men and women of all ages dressed unapologetically in synthetic blends focusing hard on the cards and wheels and dice in front of them while grinning green-aproned Caucasians ran around administering exchanges and delivering soft drinks. Alcohol was not present in these big bright rooms, but high faith was everywhere, shining stubbornly from everyone's eyes. I never learned blackjack or how to place an off-track bet, but stuck with five-card draw, the only thing I knew, and at the end of each evening when people dimmed down and turned philosophical I commiserated with Jim, a widowed Maine lobsterman visiting his married girlfriend during the off-season. When I told him about the librarian he said, "Sounds like his bullshit's getting in the way of his slow-moving dream," and when I told him I was trying to make a decision about whether to stay, he cut me off with scorn, saying, "Nope, nope, I don't buy it, you don't *try to make* a decision, I mean, you don't *try to make* a decision. You know what you want to do. You do what you want to do."

Jim was small and shifty-eyed and his whole face and neck were gray as if they'd gone that way naturally along with his hair, but I could not ignore him, even though he often discounted himself, saying, "Hey, I'm not the first guy to talk about God while he's gambling and I won't be the last." So I listened and moved to Florida, where Jim had grown up happily, he said, stealing canoes and blowing up cypress knees with homemade gasoline bombs, and where I'd always imagined myself in cutoffs someday. I was in Florida no more than a week before I went to the Round Bar, where Jim claimed to have seen a girl bare her tattooed breasts one night before the pink light of the jukebox; it was either George Jones or Waylon Jennings playing, he recalled, and she was dancing and crying, and then she just pulled up her T-shirt, and on her left tit it said BORN TO RIDE, RIDE TO DIE and on her right tit it said TIT.

"Of course that was twelve, fifteen years ago," Jim said. "Place may not even be open anymore." But when I got there it was and nothing had changed: elephant ears hid the door, cats slept on the windowsills, antique beer signs blinked on the walls over the splitting leather booths, and the big bar rotated endlessly, imperceptibly, in the center of the room, just as he'd described, as though nothing in the world had changed, as though time and distance meant nothing. "Drop me a line if you ever make it there," Jim had said, but the singer was playing the first night I went, and after that I just never got around to it.

• • •

Tonight is the singer's last night. Tomorrow he'll be back in Nashville trying to sell his songs, back with his wife and his wife's cat and his new baby Liza and his four teenage sons from his first marriage. But watching him it is impossible to believe that he won't be here tomorrow, that he hasn't always been here. He's set up on his stool on a wood pallet just large enough for him and his bass pedals and the one Wellington he's taken off in order to play them, big black Peavey behind his elbow like another person, his head angling with the words like he's kissing someone, and the music, what he calls his "fat" sound, pouring out of him, high clean string notes and his fat serious voice together filling the round round room, beautiful.

"Aw, he's not *that* good," Ron Russell says. He and his brother have joined me in my booth and are trying to convince me to take a ride in their Mr. Small Dent wrecker truck so that I'll stop paying attention to the singer and pay attention to them.

"He does got a sweet mouth on him, I will say that much," Jeff Russell says.

"I can show her something better than that," Ron says.

"Hey, look at yerself," Jeff says to Ron. "*Look* at yerself. Not a very pretty picture, is it?"

"I think Ron is a good-looking guy," I say.

"You hear that?" Jeff shouts.

"Aw, she's in love," Ron says. "She ain't taken her eyes off him for one second. Not *one second*."

And that's true. The singer strums hard, letting loose the strong sad first chords of "Seminole Wind," sending them flying like wild heavy birds into the room. "What he's got is a *gift*," Jeff says, his eyes on the singer, and his oil-dirty face appears both older and younger than it was a moment ago. "God gave that boy a gift."

"Gift, right," his brother says. "Listen. Picasso? Van Gogh? They was just assholes who *presented* theirselves as important."

Still, I cannot get close enough to the singer. When we embrace, my arms go over his shoulders, around his head, and his big stomach presses into the area that starts at my belly and goes down to the middle of my thighs. His stomach is hard and creates a certain space between us; his small legs in their Wranglers seem far, far away. And even in bed he always leaves his socks on because his feet were ruined standing in the swamp in Cambodia; other Marines had cush duty, he says, but he was in the swamp, always in the swamp, in fact he was a sharpshooter, *in fact* he can say with almost complete certainty that it was his bullet that killed Baby Doc Duvalier's right-hand man. The few times he's taken them off, I've forgotten to look. And though he chain-smokes Dorals, he is odorless. His dick is small and in the morning when he's gone nothing's sore and nothing smells. Lying down he is a big man who yells, who *growls* in bed, but he leaves before it gets light and nothing is left behind, as though all the hair, the sweat, all the *man* of him has gone into his music-playing, soaked up by the Round Bar's fat old cypress walls.

"I want . . ." I sometimes say to him in bed, but I don't know how to finish the sentence. He thinks I'm talking about being unemployed and starts taking dollars out of his wallet for me. I lie there full of desperate, dead-end feelings, a big useless naked girl, an idiot savant. "My dear," he says, looking me up and down, "being with you is like Saturday night at the movies for a guy like me." I want something impossible. I want to dance with him to the music he plays. I want to look over his shoulder, feel him solid in my arms, his baby-smelling beard against my throat, but see him set up in the corner at the same moment singing *Love is like a dying ember, only memories remain; through the ages I'll remember . . .* I want to go to Nashville.

A tall man who looks like Jesus or Willie Nelson makes his way over to me, extends his long arm. "Sorry, sir, she cain't dance," Ron says. "She's waiting on her boyfriend over there."

"Fair enough," the Jesus man says. "You're pretty," he says to me. Then he goes over to the tiny, salt-sprinkled dance floor and hops up and down there beside the jukebox's pink light, keeping his back straight and kicking and stomping his feet, four fat women dancing around him, all of them doing the same steps and keeping perfect time, all of them smiling. "I fell for you like a child," the singer sings. "I fell into a burning ring of fire." Watching him, I know what I must do; for once I am spared the shame of decision-making. I dig through my purse for my keys, already picturing which panties to pack, which earrings and shoes, already hearing myself on the phone to my father, asking to borrow just a couple hundred, telling him, *Yes, I have several different projects lined up, various possibilities right now, yes, many paths are still open to me.*

• • •

In the deep end of the Nashville Sheraton's pool, a young girl will not stop watching me. She is the only child in the pool, and I stare back at her, wondering if I know her from somewhere. But no, I think, I don't know any children. Despite the drought, the pool's water level is too high, and I'm hanging on the side with the other adults, all of us sipping drinks from plastic cups and holding our heads at unnatural angles, trying to appear relaxed. The girl floats near me on her stomach on a neon-patterned raft, chewing the ends of her long brown hair and watching me, staring as though she wants to know something. "Why are you looking at me?" she asks finally.

"I'm not," I say. I stare at her body laid out flat in a maroon one-piece, the small but unequivocal curves of her long legs and short torso.

"Where's your husband?" she asks.

"Don't have one."

"Oh," she says. She thinks. "I thought I saw this man looking at me before," she says.

I swallow the last inch of my red wine, which is hot as coffee, and squint up into the bewildering light. The girl is not going away.

"I like your hair," she says. She grins shyly and undulates like a fish, making the raft move closer.

Okay, I think. "I have to go upstairs and get ready," I tell her. "Would you like to come up to my room with me and watch TV?" She nods and undulates, her small round behind rising and falling in the waves she makes.

My phone's message light still isn't blinking. "Would you like a soda or something?" I ask the girl. She looks at the carafe of wine on the table. "How old are you?" I say. She blushes, pulls on the wet ends of her hair. "It's okay," I say, taking the paper crown off a glass and handing it to her. "What are you, eleven? You're twelve?" I pour her a little more.

"Can I look in your bathroom?" she says.

"Go ahead, I've got some calls to make," I say. I call the hotel switchboard and ask the operator to recheck my voice mail. Then I call the singer's double-wide but hang up when he answers. Finally I call my own number in Florida and listen to the messages on my machine. Jeff Russell wants to know if I'll be at the Round Bar tonight. "I'm hoping against hope," he says. Sally from Live Oak Office Supply has my resumé and wants to set up an interview right away. The librarian is sending me a book that made him think of me, something about the "cultural wasteland of the South." "Ciao, baby," he says, his voice the same old sly whisper.

"Do you have anyone you need to call?" I ask the girl when she comes out of the bathroom.

"Yeah, my brother," she says. "He has epilepsy. He's eighteen but he can't be in the room alone 'cause he might crack his skull open, like on the edge of the desk. Do you have any brothers or sisters?"

I shake my head and lie down on one of the beds, exhausted from the sun. With my eyes shut I can again hear the singer on the phone, saying, "You know if I had my choice I'd be with you," his wife's cat crying in the background, his baby crying right into the phone, in his arms, it sounded like. "You know, you have a certain spiritual quality," he said. "Have we worked anything out?" I asked, confused. "No, but we will," he said. "I'll be in touch." Now it occurs to me that he never asked for my room extension. Does he remember my last name? I wonder.

The girl speaks in soft monosyllables, sitting in her damp suit on a towel on the other bed, her feet on the floor and her back straight, reminding me of Jesus and his four girlfriends dancing at the Round Bar, which at the moment seems impossibly far away, a dark room somewhere on some darker, dirtier side of the planet. Her glass, on the nightstand, is already empty. "I'm sad about my dog," she says after she hangs up.

"Go get him," I suggest.

"No, *she*," she says. "She's in Conyers but I don't think she's going to remember me when we get back. My dad said the first night she acted like she saw a ghost in the hamper but now she's acting fine."

"How long are you here for?" I ask.

"Um, I don't know. My aunt has a tilted uterus and we have to wait. Can we watch 'Muppet Babies'?" I toss her the remote. "Can I come over tomorrow?" she says.

"Sure," I say. "Listen, is your dog big or small?"

"Big. Like this high."

"Because I don't know about small dogs, but I think if she's a good big dog she'll remember you when she sees you. She won't know what happened exactly, but she'll have this feeling that something was wrong but now it's better. She'll feel happier than usual, kind of desperately happy, you know what I mean?

Like she won't remember having ever felt so happy to see you, but she won't know why. Behind being happy there'll just be this *loss*, only she won't quite remember what the loss was, like a dream that leaves you with a feeling but you can't remember the dream, you know?"

"Yeah," the girl says.

"Do you want to order something?" I say. "Order anything you want."

She leaves when it gets dark and I pull myself together, putting on rings and perfume and eyeshadow; the bathroom has a new foul smell and so I close it off and use the mirror over the dresser. At nine-thirty I try the double-wide again and hang up when his wife says hello. I lie on the bed in my jeans and fringed jacket and watch a special about ghost sightings in small Southern towns where Civil War battles are known to have taken place. "Were you here during the war?" an old lady with a tape recorder asks the air over the banks of a river in the middle of the night. Amid static and the rushing of water on the playback a faint moaning is amplified: "Mm mmm *mmm* mmmmm," and a transcription runs across the bottom of the screen: "I was *in* the war . . . I was *in* the war."

At two or three I wake up rolling over, my boot heels knocking together, and reach for the phone, which hasn't rung. In the dark I listen again to Jeff Russell, Sally, and the librarian, and now a new one, a distant, familiar voice like an all-night DJ: "I don't know if you remember me, I met you back in California, back last winter in the desert with all those Indians, remember we had that lucky pink dauber at Bingo? I had the blue truck and the red motorcycle, gave you a ride a couple times, I was Jim . . . Well, I'm back on the maritime coast of Maine and business is booming, weather's good, and sometimes I just start flipping through the old Rolodex and goddamn, whatever happened to everyone? I hope I have the right number here. I just wanted to touch base, you know, see what's up, see if you ever made it out there to that goddamned rotating bar. Man, goddamn rotating bar! I remember one night I was just *poached*, Country Whiskey Shot Night, it was, and I was talking to a girl, talking her up, buying highballs, pretty girl, and then I go to the bathroom and when I come back she's gone! I started talking to her but when I looked a great big muley fucking *cowboy's* in her place. Turns out she's halfway around the room already, a hundred and goddamn eighty degrees away. *Goddamn* rotating bar! She was there one minute and then she was gone. Boy, what I put up with from women, all in the name of perfume! Nice girl, too. I always wondered what became of her . . ."

On and on he talks, and when the tape runs out, cutting him off, I punch my code and listen to it all again, hugging the phone to my head like a stuffed animal, and again, until I fall asleep, and wake up because a waiter is pounding on the door, the same pimply, red-haired waiter who brought me the wine yesterday, only now he's checking to make sure I'm okay, since the phone was off the hook so long. "Sorry to disturb you, miss, it's just policy," he says, and I ask him for another carafe, but he says the bar isn't open yet, not until noon, but he can put my order in now if I want. "Oh, no need, that's okay," I tell him, "I'm fine, thanks anyway."

My face is swollen, my hair a sad tangle, my eyes swim in iridescent hollows of Revlon Indian Summer Dusk. It seems there is someone I should be calling, but it's Saturday, too late for Sally at Live Oak Office Supply, and I can't imagine calling the librarian, can't imagine that I ever spoke to him or would want to speak to him again, and Jim, Jim I would talk to but somehow in his whole message he never got around to saying his number, or maybe he said it after the tape ended and the number's still sitting out there in the air somewhere, floating somewhere between Maine and here, unreachable. I wish there were a way to phone the Round Bar, not to speak to anyone in particular but just to pass the time of day, as though you could just call up a place like it were a person and say, "Hey there, how are you doing? You know I've been thinking about you a lot lately, you know you're never far from my thoughts."

The girl arrives at ten in her suit but she doesn't want to go swimming. "It's too crowded," she says. We step onto the balcony into the bright sun and gaze down at the pool, which I notice for the first time is the empty bean shape. The shallow end is crowded with little girls from some camp or club tossing Barbie heads to each other and singing *This is the song that never ends, it goes on and on, my friend* . . . "Last night I had the weirdest dream," the girl says. "I was in *The Muppet Movie*, and I was in this relay race, only instead of a baton we were passing a towel. My friend Heather was wearing metal shorts that were really a pan, a lead pan. Do you, um, have any more wine?" she asks.

"I'm working on it," I tell her.

She sits with one leg tucked under her on the unmade bed and watches herself in the mirror, assuming several uncertain postures. She has the pensive look again, the one she had in the pool. "I'm sorry if I made your bathroom smell," she says finally.

"I didn't notice," I say.

"See, I have polyps," she says.

"That must hurt," I say after a while.

"Yeah," she says. "I had an operation when I was six, eight, nine, and last year on Columbus Day. It hurts when I get nervous."

"What do you get nervous about?" I ask.

"Like, if I'm waiting for something to happen, or like, now talking about it, it hurts, but that's all in my head, I'm supposed to use mind over matter." I stare at her stomach, smooth and shimmery under lycra and no bigger than an appetizer plate but hiding such treachery and dissent. *The only time I feel the pain, is in the sunshine and the rain*, I think. "Excuse me," the girl says, with sudden tears, and runs to the bathroom.

I turn the TV on loud, Geraldo, and almost don't hear the knock. The singer is a pale Martian in the light of day, a strangely solid ghost. "Hello, my dear," he says in his soft, lying voice. *I love you*, I think, and say nothing. He steps inside, a short fat man in a tractor cap, and sits at the table, a stranger.

He talks about the tape I've asked him so many times to make for me, says he'll send it soon, his brother is moving to Nashville soon and when he does they're going to build a house, and in the basement will be a recording studio, and the sound will be perfect, it will all happen soon. "You do what you want to do," I say. Sitting across from him I don't want him to touch me, but when he does, reaching over and laying his warm square palm on my cheek and holding it there, his bicep swelling under his rolled sleeve, I cannot pull away, it has been so long, something like my whole life, since anyone's touched me. "This isn't a good idea," I say, and he says, "I've lost a lot of things in my life, but I regret nothing more than losing you," and I think, *Your bullshit's getting in the way of your slow-moving dream*, but still I cannot pull away.

He moves me to the bed easily, matter-of-factly, like switching guitars between songs, and there does what he has always done, making me feel that there's something I'm forgetting, something important, something beautiful, but I can't quite get it, it's leaving me, leaving me like a dream. With my eyes closed against his shoulder I hear her voice, a soft echo in my head, as though she's hiding there and not in the bathroom. *Wait*, she says. "Wait," I say, but my voice has no force and he doesn't wait, he goes on. He won't stay for long, I answer her silently; he has never stayed for long. And when he leaves he never says when he's coming back. *Goodbye, sweetheart.* Holding him, I can feel the words in him already, before they hit the air. *Please wait*, I plead with her in my head. *He is almost gone.*

She does not come out of the bathroom. When he's gone I sit naked where he's left me, feeling myself sweat, keeping my head turned away from the dresser mirror. *Look at yourself. Look at yourself. Not a very pretty picture, is it?*

The bathroom is silent, the door blank and white. "Are you okay in there?" I call. There's no sound, not even water, not even rustling. "Hello, are you all right? Hello, say something!" The doorknob is cold and I jiggle it hard, as though trying to revive it.

"No, don't come in!" she says.

"It's okay," I tell her, speaking through the door. I sit down on the carpet there, pulling the corner of the sheet from the bed around myself and leaning my face against the cool white wall. "You can come out whenever you're ready, okay?" I tell her. "It's safe now, so just come out whenever you're ready. No one will hurt you, I promise."

brighten her work space she tacks up photos of men who remind her of Joe, the man she is in love with. There's Jack Nicholson, a local talk show host, and an unidentified magician from an ad for vodka. It's not that she doesn't have photos of Joe himself, but there's something exciting, amazing even, about finding his likeness in someone else. Connection is implied, connection and fate. Her co-workers needle her about this; a divorced editor named Jan, in particular, takes issue with Helene in a smilingly sardonic way. "Do you actually *believe* this zodiac stuff?" she says.

"No," Helene says quickly. "It's just exciting to think that there's a connection, however random . . ."

"But why can't it be just as exciting," Jan says, "to think that there's no connection at all? That's what *I* call exciting."

Helene has no answer for this, but on the whole she feels lucky to be part of the close, energetic crew of people at this company. Outside of work she feels a little unanchored. But at the office, for eight and a half hours each day, even though her mind starts to repeat itself as she labels, counts, and copies, she is secure in ritual.

Joe is twelve years older than Helene, between jobs but unalarmed. He literally doesn't sweat over things. His body barely even has a scent of its own, beyond soap. Helene thinks this is because he refuses to move fast enough to perspire. It's a small rebellion of his; he seems exempt from the rush of city living, but really his spirit gets by, undiluted, sneaking around in his slow body. He still believes, in his late thirties, that he can get away with whatever he pleases. He lets his spine hang in a lazy posture of truth, for anyone who cares to notice, and of course Helene notices. Joe has a favorite, comical houseplant, a dimestore jade tree, that he claims reminds him of her. The plant fell apart once when he repotted it, but now it grows so rapidly it seems to stretch upward before his very eyes, with the same awkwardness Helene seems to suffer when she's over at his place, trying so hard to act offhand. He says he expects someday to catch her stumbling around in a pair of dress-up pumps three sizes too large.

They met at O'Hare International, in a cocktail lounge where a small crowd was waiting out a blizzard. It was just before Christmas, and the low-ceilinged room was dimly lit with strung bulbs. Everyone in the lounge was watching a news program on the wall television about a woman who'd been trapped under a piece of construction machinery for seven hours, but who'd lived and learned to walk again. People were turning to each other over their drinks to exclaim about this miracle. An airline worker wearing a weighty jumpsuit sat next to Helene. "I know of a club about a mile from here," he said softly. "It only costs three bucks to get in and they got a pool that's hot as a bathtub." Helene nodded and kept her eyes on the TV. The airline worker shrugged and started telling her about his father, who'd died recently in an auto wreck. "It's just plain hard," he said. "You only get one father."

Helene tried to think if anything this difficult had ever happened to her, but nothing had. Her parents were clever agnostics who didn't believe in sadness or the unknown. Her mother, for instance, could tell you what they'd be having for dinner three weeks from now. Helene imagined that when it was her parents' time to die they would manage to make a rational decision out of it somehow, just as they chose what vegetable went with pork chops or what color carpeting to put in Helene's old bedroom when she moved out. Unreasonable occurrences such as auto wrecks kept their distance from Helene's parents. On the other hand, so did miracles. For that matter, so did Helene. The airline worker was still watching her hopefully. She coughed and turned away, and there sat Joe on her other side, looking ageless and arch and familiar. He gazed at her as though he'd been gazing at her on and off for years.

"If you think that's bad," he said finally, "listen to what happened to me. I went to buy a goldfish this morning and the bus I was on ran right over a cat. Broad daylight. Killed it." Helene felt her face fall, out of her control. "But wait," he said, "that's not all. I got to the aquarium store and it was all boarded up!

Apparently the old man who ran the place got *hit by a car*, running across the street for lunch. Can you believe it?

Helene shook her head. She couldn't tell if he was actually self-pitying or just trying to get her to talk. It seemed that he might be neither. "Well," she said, "I was at the YMCA the other day and I overheard two little girls in the locker room, and one of them said, 'You look like a woman,' and the other one said, 'I do?' and the first one said, 'Yeah.' It was wild." Helene knew she was striving for non sequitur. Joe looked surprised and slightly touched. They exchanged names and she took note of his bad complexion and the precise way his lips came together. "Are you waiting for a plane?" she asked. Her own flight was grounded, not because of the blizzard, but mechanical trouble.

"I'm trying to get out of the country," Joe said. Helene noticed his dark whiskers, dark lashes. "I'm on standby for half a dozen flights," he said. "Anywhere warm. And you? Wait—let me guess. You're a college student, right? Home to the folks for Christmas? No—I'll bet you're going to Palm Beach with five friends who look exactly like you, only blonder, right?

"Well, close," Helene said. "Phoenix. But I'm not a student." She was making her yearly visit to an old high school friend whose parents ran a guest ranch.

"Always good to get away for the holidays," Joe said. "Go somewhere hot and foreign, where people don't get so worked up."

Helene sipped her vodka and 7-Up and silently agreed. She loved the tropical, slowed-down feel of life at her friend's ranch, even though she knew it was inauthentic, produced by a paid staff for the tourists. There was something, nevertheless, about the palmettos and prickly pears and the birds that ran up and down on the footpaths that seemed to mock the guests and all their serious human activities. Helene supposed if you grew up surrounded by these crazy plants and wild pigs and coyotes howling like sirens in the night you might not feel so starved for extremity. You might just calm down and get on with your life. At any rate, she always came back to the Midwest. She had to admit that what she loved about Arizona was probably only the novelty; you couldn't base your whole life on what the foliage happened to look like. "So what do you do for a living?" she asked Joe.

He told her he was the voice of time; he had made a local telephone time recording. They'd paid him a fortune for that, he said, and before that he had worked in a burlap bag factory that burned to the ground. He wore a stylish double-breasted suit, Helene saw, and he took his cigarette smoke up through his nostrils. "Are you also an artist?" she asked.

"Oh, Christ, no," he said.

Embarrassed, Helene glanced at the TV, on which an interviewer was now leaning forward toward his guest, saying, "So, do women *dig* conflict?" "You know," Helene said, "I don't go around picking up men in bars."

"Don't sweat it," Joe said. "You think innocents are any more *pure* than we are?" He paused dreamily for a moment, then said, "You're just a little something God sent me."

No one had ever said anything like that to Helene. She slid her napkin out from under her glass immediately and got a pen out of her bag and wrote down her phone number for Joe. When her flight was announced he kissed her on the forehead and wished her good luck back at college. She was halfway down the long corridor to her gate, her heart pounding, before she realized she hadn't corrected him. She thought of a phrase from one of the astrology guides she'd worked on: *When the student is ready, the teacher arrives.* At the gate a group of noisy, bright-jacketed teens were jittering around restlessly, clutching homemade posters that read WELCOME HOME, AMBER!! IF YOU'RE TAN, JUST GO BACK!!! I was never that cynical, Helene thought. I don't ever want to be that cynical.

Before Joe, Helene had only one other boyfriend. He was younger than Joe and much more ambitious. His life's work, he knew at twenty-five, was in the public sector. He was very principled about certain things. He made Helene feel ridiculously important and minuscule at the same time. "I'm so proud of you," he'd say to her, "with that little job of yours." Once they had an argument which ended with him standing over her, kicking her in the side. The argument started over a TV program Helene liked, and ended with him shouting at her that she must learn to live in the real world. She thought, at the time, that he was trying to help her.

Remembering that time in her life makes Helene's stomach turn as though the earth has suddenly reversed in its orbit. She wishes she could pull the rug out from underneath her memories. She is smart enough to know about things like taking charge, responsibility, Oprah Winfrey, about independence being the redemption of the modern woman. But certain of her longings she cannot seem to eliminate. She would just like to *locate* her faith, get it down to a science, like packing her lunch each night. Jan, at work, seems disgusted with her. "You know what you need to work on?" she asks Helene rhetorically. "Your relationship with your*self*." Another of Jan's favorites is: "We all cause our own happiness and unhappiness, and the sooner you accept that, the better." But Jan might as well be from Mars as far as Helene is concerned. She lives alone, Helene knows, and is constantly modifying her diet, eliminating sugar, adding brown rice, as though health is a mountain that need only be climbed, as though appetite is of no consequence whatsoever. She is active in small political organizations that support distant and obscure causes, and she often urges Helene to "get outside" herself and come to a protest or a rally. At the office, Jan snaps Polaroids at parties, keeps the money for the football pool, and gets mildly involved in everybody's business. Helene supposes she herself is too self-involved, too busy tallying, stockpiling, looking for various affirmations, to get up much steam for Jan's type of activities. She supposes Jan has a point. Helene is, after all, tired of so much craving.

Early one morning, an unassuming spring dawn, Helene gets up and goes into Joe's chilly bathroom. She has slept at his apartment only two or three times so far. There on the edge of the sink sits his bar of soap, plastered with dark short hairs from his head. She feels like she's seen his diary, or a hidden scar; she can't believe his body let this happen. She can't believe the soap let this happen. She can't believe she's allowed to see this. By the time she tiptoes back into the bedroom it is filled with light. She eases under the comforter, unsure if Joe is conscious. "What happened to you?" he mumbles.

"I found salvation in your bathroom," she says, trying to make it sound like a joke. She watches Joe slip so easily back into sleep, and quiets her heart, trying, as hard as she's ever tried anything, to match his slow deep breathing.

• • •

Joe has been engaged to be married twice in his life. The first time was to a precocious girl who wanted him to help her hold up a Circle K store just outside of Amarillo. He didn't go through with that plan, but they did drive all over Texas together in a Vega loaded with half-empty liquor bottles and assorted ammunition. Every town they stopped in they charmed people. The girl wore a football jersey that said "Mikey" on the back, and Joe wore a string tie that fastened with an enormous lump of turquoise. Men in filling stations kept calling him "Mikey" when he paid for gas. Eventually, the girl decided to go back to school, and made this clear to Joe one night by throwing a folding chair at his head. He recovered and met an internationally known runway model at a party in Houston where he tended bar. The model's father was a Nigerian statesman who had survived the revolution there, money intact. He seemed to like Joe's offhand wit, or perhaps his taste in clothing; at any rate, it was decided that Joe would marry the runway model, who was actually only seventeen. This engagement lasted three weeks and then the model shaved her head and tried to shoot her father. Her father bought Joe a one-way plane ticket to a Northern city. This was all going on in Joe's life at the same time Helene was a ten-year-old making God's eyes out of yarn and sticks at summer camp.

Joe doesn't recall the exact moment he first laid eyes on Helene, or anyone else, for that matter. It's been a long, long time since he was surprised at the way people entered and exited his life. Some people might even consider him detached—a doctor once told him: You refuse to dip your toe in the stream running right outside your own front door. It's unfortunate, but that's how it is. There are a thousand ways to get by, Joe knows, and nine hundred and ninety-nine of them involve messing other people up. Truthfully, he doesn't feel unfortunate at all. One thing he's noticed is that if there's anything worse than bad memories, it's the insidious good ones. Remembering too far back makes his heart feel like a balled-up washcloth. His heart hurts, his head aches, it hurts to look out the window and smell October coming. Who needs that kind of pain? Not Joe, who once stood on the roof of the Sears Tower wearing only a loincloth, and another time served paella to Natalie Wood. When you let go, life is one fabulous day at a time.

He wishes Helene could learn to relax, though he doesn't see it as his business to teach her. He wishes she wouldn't think about their ages. He knows she thinks a lot about loving him, what it means to love him, and he wishes she wouldn't. His love for her isn't anything he thinks about; it's like a birthmark— he would never doubt its permanence. One night he broiled a chicken for their dinner, and when he cut half from his plate for her she stared at him so intensely he told her to stop it, she was being too romantic about the whole thing. But this was a mistake; he doesn't want to tell her how to act. He would no more patronize her than patronize his own big toe. "Think about moving in with me," he says. When he sees her expression, he says, not unkindly, "Jesus, here we go." But then she laughs, and he thinks: *Maybe there is hope.* He can't focus on all her fears, all her trying, who she thinks she is or who she tries so hard to be. He sees only Helene, and senses the inevitable unknown, waiting, as it always does, for the right moment. Which is okay with Joe, because he can wait forever.

• • •

Summer is over, and Helene is not sleeping well. She wakes up in the middle of the night and believes she is missing a self. She's positive there were two, and now there's only air next to her in the bed. One is supposed to be the child, and one the woman. Which one is still here? She hasn't decided whether or not to move in with Joe, and it's driving her nuts. During the day she rushes impatiently through her rituals; she spends less time on her hair, less time at lunch, and less time actually working. She finds ways to streamline, to take shortcuts in her work. She is definitely hurrying, but hurrying toward what?

"You sure are jumpy," Jan says.

"I know it," Helene says. "If I could just figure out what to do about the Joe situation . . ."

"Oh, situation schmituation!" Jan says. "You're still *in* love with him."

"What are you talking about?" Helene says.

"You've got to get past *that*, if it's going to work," says Jan. "Every relationship should have its disillusionment." She picks nonchalantly at the edge of Helene's desk blotter.

Helene is suddenly annoyed. "There's a big difference between you and me," she says. "You're divorced!"

"The difference between you and me," Jan says, "is that I know how to have a good time."

Lately Joe has been suggesting that they shop for furniture, but Helene has a revelation: she suggests they go buy that goldfish he's been wanting. They drive way out in the west suburbs on a mild Saturday in September. The day is clear and warm, but rather fainthearted—the smell of fall is everywhere. They drive so far they have to pay three tolls. From the outside the Pet Castle looks like a regular building, but inside the decor is lush and confusing. Neither Joe nor Helene has ever seen anything like it; it looks like both an enchanted forest and a Swiss chalet. Walnut beams crisscross overhead, and a waterfall rushes down from the second level. Tropical birds scream from the rafters, and the pond is crowded with goldfish. Joe looks disappointed.

"What is it?" Helene asks.

"I don't know," he says glumly. "In a setup like this, they can never catch the one you want."

"Maybe they'll let you catch it yourself," she says. "Do you know what you're going to name it?" She's assumed Joe is the kind of person who comes up with witty names for pets.

"Nothing at all," Joe says. "If you name them, they just die. That's the whole secret behind goldfish."

Helene nods and walks away so he won't see her looking taken aback. She squeezes between customers and rows of cages. Excited children keep bumping into her.

An animated woman with a tiny terrier under her arm is chatting with a salesperson. "My puppy's fine now," Helene overhears. "The instant we get in the car, he just goes right to sleep." The salesperson nods vigorously. "That's as it should be," he says with a heavy European accent.

Helene finds the kittens, her favorites. There are at least twenty of them, squirming and crying in a big glass showcase lined with newspaper. They climb all over each other trying to get close to her. She sees one kitten step right on another kitten's face. This is not a good advertisement for cohabitation, she thinks. The European salesperson arrives at her side and says, "You want to hold?"

"Oh, no thanks," she says. It would just make it impossible. Once she held it, she'd have to keep it. And she doesn't even know where she'll be living in one month's time. If only they were literate, Helene thinks suddenly. She wouldn't mind having a pen-pal here at the Pet Castle. But what could you write to a kitten? How would you explain to it why it couldn't come live with you? The salesperson wanders off and the kittens mew frantically. Helene wonders if they are as innocent as they appear to be. "I doubt it," she says aloud.

From behind her, a small raspy voice says: "I doubt it."

She whirls around, and there's a smug black myna bird on a perch. "What the hell," she says. The bird edges toward her, then edges back. "Tell me something else," Helene says, but the bird is silent. It bobs its head, shakes out its shiny black wings, lifts its feet and sets them down, one small round eye trained on Helene. It is definitely telling her something, but what, *what*? But maybe its strange movements are enough; maybe this, the fact that she and the bird are speaking to each other, is all she is supposed to know. She turns and sees Joe up on the second level, grinning at her and waving a goldfish in a plastic bag. Maybe this is what life will be like with him, she thinks. One small miracle after another.

the oysters

Pat Boone—not *the* Pat Boone but only a graduate student in Agricultural Science—was driving the oysters down to Mulberry to have them irradiated. He was used to being the wrong Pat Boone but was nevertheless miserable, careening down Interstate 75 in the windless predawn, gripping the wheel of the Food Science van with his troubled pink fingers. He thought he might have a fever; he kept sneezing and his freckles kept getting in his eyes like gnats, reflecting off his pale face and blinding him. He whizzed past lit signs and enticements, antic neon red coffee cups with legs flashing on and off, simulating dancing, and bold messages in balloons above them urging him to WAKE UP. He was awake but dreaming, dreaming of Maura Malone. He saw bits of her—breast, hand, thigh—but none were what he wanted, or, wanting them, he only wanted more. To be awake at this hour was to be unable to see Maura's marriage as hypothetical.

Keep your mind on the oysters, he told himself. He had two, almost three degrees. He believed the unknown was simply a subset of the known; he expected, logically, the unexpected. The oysters were packed in dry ice in ten bushel cartons, sitting like obedient campers on the long van seats behind him, the first live food items ever to be irradiated. The preservation process was new, not yet commercialized, and on local news programs almost nightly angry college students and young mothers could be seen protesting, mildly scornful doctors and scientists rebutting. Month-old irradiated strawberries that looked and tasted fresh had just arrived on the market; grocery shoppers were videotaped sampling and appraising them. Farmers both excited and skeptical were shown standing in their groves, making thrilling and dire predictions about their industry. The oysters were the biggest story yet; as a representative of his department, Pat would be a part of history. He had twice been interviewed on the evening news, and the *Tampa Tribune* woman was going to meet him at the plant in Mulberry. In twenty-four hours people up and down the Florida coast would begin commenting to one another over their English muffins about his funny name.

But Maura, Maura slept beside her husband even now: her large tropical husband with his flourishing mustache, not the kind you hid behind but the kind you cultivated with cheerful, automatic faith, the way you would plant a vegetable garden or have children. Pat had met the man at bars and buffet tables many times and found him unbearable. "I'm Trinidadian," he'd told Pat once, "and we sing when we talk." The Trinidadian's smile was so open and precious that it made a small sound, breaking out upon his large, honest face. Pat shook the sound out of his head and drove sneezing and invisible down the dark and empty highway.

In a recent *Food Science Newsletter* feature story Maura had claimed to have known within twenty minutes of meeting the Trinidadian that he was "the one." The photo showed her standing glamorously beside the Gammacell 220 as though it were a sewing machine she was about to demonstrate. She wore her white coat and held a pint of strawberries she was preparing to feed into the irradiator, the hard fluorescent lab lights making her sleek, tightly bound-up hair appear glossy and beautiful. "Professor Malone operates our own modest machine," the caption read.

Pat clenched the vibrating steering wheel with both hands as though it alone could save him. *He* had known within twenty minutes of entering Maura's classroom that *she* was the one. In a year he had thought this a thousand times, and had even known enough not to say it aloud, known that not saying it was the way to sustain it. But surely the eerie, thrilling consummation of his feelings, her finally humming in the familiar hiss of his shower or standing at his range scrambling eggs as casually as a ghost—surely these things were proof of their love's inevitability. He had *known* it. Her words in the interview caused him a shocking, embarrassing kind of pain, as though someone had without warning ripped a Band-Aid off his heart. He could not bear to think of the Trinidadian sashaying around so happily unconscious, the way he himself must have looked before he met her. He could not even remember what he'd spent time thinking about before he met her. His own mind, his own heart, before Maura, were lost to him.

He tried as a game to imagine the oysters as cheerful children in his charge, giddy prodigies eager to take part in such a significant experiment, but this was just fantasy and he couldn't sustain it. Instead he recalled something he hadn't thought about in years, a childhood vacation on Sanibel Island which he and his brothers had spent feverishly collecting the best whelks and scallops and periwinkles, the rare ones with the live creatures still in them. They took dozens back to their room at the Jolly Roger each afternoon to be boiled on the hot plate, never tiring of watching the mysterious blobs spreading out over the bottom of the pot, the strange sightless animals surrendering in their rubbery, milky puddles. The sexy, velvety smell of the mineral oil they'd used to polish the empty shells came back to him, carrying with it a surge of the old wonder, the nameless thrill of boiling the sea creatures.

But the oysters behind him now were cold and silent and clamped shut, hiding their secrets. His life seemed small and doomed and embarrassing, and the loop of time between his days at the Jolly Roger and the present seemed like someone's, maybe Maura's, idea of a good joke. How Maura could be responsible for the sad loop of his life he could not explain.

I am not invisible, he told himself, his eyes blurring. *I exist*. He wanted to state these things out loud to someone, someone in a position of authority, but he had only himself to address.

• • •

Ebb and flow, stir and settle, bubble and curl. This was what the oysters knew. But now they sensed a change. Something was happening. Of course, they had known everything that would ever happen to them from the moment they had come into existence, from even before they had existed, but they had certainly not bargained for this. Excitement was in the air. A new element hissed around them like a predator. Beneath them rumbled more than the usual uncomfortable earth. They stirred thickly in their shells, uncertain.

• • •

The month-old strawberries, for their part, resented that they were not considered to be "live." They understood, in their pungent, opaque way, that life was romance. They had played an important part in more than one courtship. Around them almost always the air harbored human hopes and celebration, or at least appreciation. They knew enjoyment. They knew ceremony. If they were not "live," what was? A machine had once been invented to measure their cries when they were bitten into.

Another machine recorded and amplified the sounds of insects eating their way through the strawberries' viscera. Men had gotten rich off these machines, but where were these men now? Strawberries everywhere felt important and, now, cheated.

• • •

Pat pulled into the plant's back lot and rolled down a window to clear, expectant tropical air. The sky was yellowing up for morning and the swampy, froggy smell of north Florida seemed far away. He backed the van up to the loading dock, thinking of Maura's Indian ringneck parakeet, who imitated the backing-up beep of her neighborhood's garbage truck. The bird was retarded, Maura said; all it did was yell nonsense words and sing over and over what it had learned of "Yankee Doodle Dandy": "I'm a doo." Sometimes when the Trinidadian was out Maura phoned and Pat could hear the bird exclaiming in the background as though it were desperate to speak to him. Once, lying unclothed in Pat's bed, holding him, Maura had told him she loved his apartment because it was as quiet as a graveyard. "Oh, thanks," he said.

"No," she said, "it's wonderful here. You're completely unencumbered."

He remembered watching her get dressed that day, feeling too moody to get up himself and see her out, but the moodiness had seemed only like love, a particularly strong swoon. She kissed him, already wearing her dark sunglasses, and said again, "I wish I had a place like this," and then darted out to her minivan and backed out of his driveway, using only her rearview mirror, not even turning her head. He remembered watching this from the window over his bed, not wanting to remove himself from the wanton crumble of sheets.

Keep your mind on the oysters! he told himself furiously.

He unloaded all ten cartons by himself, as no one appeared to greet him. Each weighed fifty pounds, and when he was finished his heart pounded with resentful diligence. If Betsy Murphy had come along, she could have helped. She was a girl in Human Nutrition whose short, strong body he'd often appraised, but he could never quite find time for her. Always Maura was there, surprising him, phoning at odd hours, blocking out more solid individuals. He stood by the locked warehouse doors, puffing in what he pictured as a cloud of his own foolishness.

A bald man in a blue jumpsuit finally threw the doors open and shook Pat's hand in both of his, apologizing steadily for being late. "You're the guest of honor," he told Pat. Pat began to feel better. Together they hoisted the wax-sealed bushels onto dollies and began wheeling them inside. "You must be tired," the man said.

"I'm all right," Pat said. The plant was only weeks old and the corridor's whitewashed cinder-block walls gleamed with promise on either side of him.

"We'll just get these babies into the holding room, and then get some coffee," the man said.

"Are you Dr. Roland?" Pat said, remembering his instructions.

The man laughed loudly, throwing back his head. "Oh, no, no," he said. "I'm no one."

• • •

The oysters furrowed and trembled, wondering. They felt themselves being moved closer to the source, but the source seemed unusual, unfamiliar. This was not the source they remembered. It was not in the oysters' nature to be suspicious, but their milky flesh curled a little. They waited, curling and subsiding. Waiting was the same as existing, for them.

• • •

The man who had invented the machine that measured the screams of fruits and vegetables was tired of waiting. He was tired of getting up every day and drinking coffee out of the same cup and waiting for purpose to come back into his life. No one had cared about his machine for years. No one cared if a tree cried when you cut it. This was the kind of thing people had cared about in the seventies. In the seventies, the man had lived in a wood-frame house that sat jauntily on stilts at the edge of the Gulf of Mexico like some happy mantis sunning itself on the beach. His smart young wife had cooked him simple, whimsical food, grits with wacky garnishes, while he worked on his important machines. His baby daughter Deenie crawled around as if motorized, her strange cries filling the airy rooms with promise and egging him on to new inventions, finer tunings. Clouds flew by overhead, hurrying to their satisfying consummations.

When had it all evaporated? It was impossible to trace. The house had long ago blown down in a brief, peevish storm too small to have been given a name. He lived now in a mildewy walk-up with his daughter, who was now a fat nurse, while his wife studied the classics in some stifling, snowbound state up north. Deenie, who could not seem to get a promotion or a boyfriend, came home from the hospital late each night and sat through one silent, reproachful beer with her father before going to bed. He stayed up later, letting the TV's false light harass his eyes, wondering what was now expected of him. Was he just supposed to sit here, waiting for people to care again, or was his purpose something else? The days rolled by, paying him no attention.

• • •

The man who had invented the machine that recorded and amplified the sounds of insects eating the insides of fruits and vegetables rode his stationary bicycle and whistled a happy tune. Agricultural and Food Science departments at universities all over the country were clamoring for his machine, and large corporations had fought one another for purchasing rights to the patent. They had paid for his stationary bike, his limestone patio, his wife's pony, his son's all-terrain vehicle, and some necessary roof repairs on the house. He puffed confidently away on his bicycle, watching through clean glass doors the steam rising off his lawn. Because of his invention, the sky would not fall on him or his family. He rarely thought of his old graduate school colleague, the man who had invented the machine that measured the screams of fruits and vegetables. That story was too sad. His own story had also been one of grief and long struggle, actually, but now that he was a success no one wanted to hear it. He was expected to shut up and be grateful, and that was what he did.

• • •

Dr. Roland was demonstrating for Pat the plywood turntable on which the oysters would ride during their irradiation. He caressed the plywood with absent, tobacco-stained fingers, gazing up at Pat with a salesman's pride and determination. "You'll want to keep an eye on those lids," he told Pat, "but otherwise feel free to circulate during the dosing."

The wax lids on the cartons would gradually yellow as they absorbed the radiation, but there would be no other visible change. A makeshift-looking motor was rigged up under the plywood to spin it, like some child's science project. The oysters, though an important part of history, did not, Pat had learned, merit treatment by the plant's showy and immense automated system. This little approximation, which might as well be a homemade microwave, was going to do the job. Pat tried not to show his disappointment. Other than its large capacity, it was no more impressive than the Gammacell back in Gainesville. What did they think he was, a Boy Scout? He scribbled figures on his pad, the minutes it would take to dose a carton with x kilograys, the total minutes he would have to keep watch. Dr. Roland stood by with neutral respect, keeping a hand on his machine. "This is quite a load of shells to haul," he said to Pat. "You order them special?"

"Nope," Pat said. "Just garden-variety Apalachicola oysters."

"Oh yes, and your reporter is here," Dr. Roland said. "She's out in the reception area whenever you're ready."

Maura was waking up now beside the Trinidadian; perhaps he sang when he awoke. A weak, sick terror took hold of Pat: what if Maura planned to visit some other student today, someone she had managed to keep secret this whole time? Then he thought of her running her hand through his own thin hair so kindly, so easily—it was impossible. It was impossible that she not love him. "Your body is perfect," she had told him. "Your body has nothing to do with reality."

"If you're wondering about safety," Dr. Roland was saying, "as well you might, let me assure you there is no cause for concern. As you'll see when you take the complete tour, there's a significantly thick concrete wall between us and the source. I just thought we'd best get started right away with these little devils in case there's a hitch. Plenty of time later to go exploring."

"Right," Pat said. He blinked and stamped his feet. "Let's go. Let's load them on."

Silent men in jumpsuits moved at Dr. Roland's command to lift the oysters onto the machine. There was nothing left for Pat to do but watch.

• • •

The insects who ate their way through fruits and vegetables did not waste time worrying about what would become of them. They knew they were romanticized by no one, and they lived accordingly, hurling themselves with abandon at mouths and ears, TV screens and lightbulbs, suns and caves. If they died, they died. On the wheel of *samsara*, they had no place to go but up. Life for them held no shame, mystery, or promise, and they did not care who spied on them or recorded them going about the business of it.

• • •

Whatever it was, it was beginning to happen. The sun itself seemed to be rotating. Each oyster sat deep in its own mystery, waiting for the shock. The shock was moments away, already sending waves back in time at them, though the waves were impossible to interpret. The air around the oysters was like music. Ordered currents began to flow. The new earth beneath them began to turn. And then the light cracked into them, and the question mark that was the world snapped itself out straight, dividing them from mystery forever.

• • •

"Back in Gainesville," Pat told the reporter, "I'd have to orient each oyster individually. Here we have the advantage of dosing whole bushels at a time. We can study both shelf-life and microbiology in one experiment."

The reporter peered at him through grass-green contact lenses, her breath smelling strongly of buttered toast. "How will you be able to tell if the oysters are dead?" she asked.

"We know they won't be dead," he said impatiently.

"But just hypothetically," she said, grinning.

He didn't see the joke, but he explained to her that any looseness in the shell was an indicator. There could be no slippage between the halves, none.

"Wow," she said.

He glanced over her shoulder at a carpeted vestibule in which was set up a courtesy telephone for guests of the plant. The phone had drawn his eyes throughout the interview, like a bomb or an unlocked safe. It shone blackly on a small table on which also sat a plate of crullers.

"What's next?" the reporter said.

"I beg your pardon?" Pat said.

"What other foods will you be working on?"

"Oh, dead chickens," Pat said, sighing.

"I can see I'm wearing you out," the reporter said, finally. She went away looking a little annoyed, her eyes somewhat dimmed.

When she was gone, Pat went and sat by the phone. He removed the pocket dosimeter from his beltloop and set it on the table beside the crullers. It was a small instrument that resembled a Sharpie pen, only with a lens at one end. Zero, it had read when he commenced the tour of the plant, and zero it read now. He had absorbed no radiation. He had penetrated wall after wall within the warehouse-sized building, moving ever closer to the source. At every new level, Dr. Roland had pointed out more buttons, more controls, more men. There were earthquake buttons and flood buttons, hurricane buttons and buttons to press if someone fell asleep. There were men whose job it was to watch buttons, and men who watched only other men. The whole thing reminded Pat of some giant child's ant-farm. He had gone as close as one could go to the great source, and his dosimeter still registered zero.

He looked again at the little instrument and thought, That's me. A big zero, coming and going. Nothing will ever change—I *am* invisible. He grabbed at the phone's receiver and punched the buttons hard, hurting his finger. *I've had it with this secret life,* he would tell her. *Keep your deceptions, your illusions, your stupid, hopeful Trinidadian. Without you my life will open up like a wonderful picture book, what people know of me will be the truth.* The phone was ringing blankly in his ear. It went on, ringing and stopping, ringing and stopping. He let his head fall for a moment and felt the blood rushing to his face like a child's hot tears. He felt like a child planning to run away from home. His courage was already dissolving, he could not sustain it. *Fine, I'll call her later*, he told himself. *From the hotel, let the University pay for it.* But even as he thought this, it was already passing out of him, going out of reach like a helium balloon. It was passing out of him and it was gone. He lifted up his head and landed back in the sweet hopelessness of his life. The oysters awaited him.

• • •

The oysters felt different, but it was difficult for them to say how. They felt as though something had been added or something taken away. They felt vaguely the urge to produce pearls, but they could not produce them. Clearly, they were leaving something behind, moving with smooth speed away from something of great importance, but what this thing was they could not remember. They felt frustrated, distracted. Where were they going? they wondered. What would happen to them? What were they supposed to do? Oh, they were only oysters! Who was there to tell their story, and who was there to listen?

the child

The child was scared of everything. She was scared of being left alone but scared of baby-sitters, especially the young ones who wore black eyeliner. The child's mother owned a tube of black eyeliner which the child could go look at anytime, sitting unassumingly in its basket on the bathroom counter, but the child wasn't scared of that. She was scared of the violent sound of her own bathwater running. When it was time for her bath, her mother would run the water and she would stay in her room with the door closed until the tub was full. But even in her room, she was scared the walls of the house would fall down. First the pictures would fall off the walls and then, a second later, the walls themselves would go, breaking apart at the corners and crashing down to the ground. She could see it so clearly, sometimes she ran fretfully from room to room, desperate for relief. Her stomach hurt when she was scared, so now she was scared of her own stomach, of its mysterious acid whims. It could start up at any moment.

"She just has a fast metabolism," the child's blasé grandmother said. The child had a blasé grandmother and a passionate grandmother. The two grandmothers sat on adjacent identical striped sofas in the living room of the child's house, watching the child practice headstands using the tripod method. They did not care for each other, though they both certainly adored the child. They lived only blocks apart, so whenever they were coming to visit the child, the blasé grandmother picked up the passionate grandmother, who didn't drive. When they arrived at the child's house, they often did not come inside immediately but could be seen sitting for minutes parked in the driveway, arguing silently behind the windshield of the blasé grandmother's sky-blue Chevy Nova.

"There's nothing wrong with the child's metabolism," the passionate grandmother told the blasé grandmother. But in her head she was not so sure. It was a fact that the child could not eat enough, could not seem to keep up her weight. What if it were true? the passionate grandmother thought. She often lay awake at night worrying about the child, and as the child grew, the grandmother's visions grew more vivid. Metabolism, my God! she thought. The child was digesting herself out of existence, evaporating by invisible increments every minute, even now, right here in front of them! The passionate grandmother stood abruptly and left the room, her eyes wild.

"Grandmother, wait, look," the child cried, in a muffled, upside-down voice.

"Back in a sec, duckie," the passionate grandmother called tremulously from the powder room. She shut herself in and sat on the fluffy blue toilet seat cover, clutching an embroidered guest towel to her stomach and imagining outrageous things. She imagined the child years from now, lost to the world, out in the dark city without grandmothers to guide her. The child would suffer flat tires, unemployment, hepatitis. In an effort to escape her parents, she would suffer any number of things. She would live in the back room of a run-down theater, eating off a hot plate and sleeping alone on a giant foam rubber pea-pod costume. The passionate grandmother could see it so clearly, she could barely catch her breath. The child was crying alone, her small sobs lost to the dark Chicago winter. The child was blindfolded and tied to a cot with Marshall Field's gold Christmas package string, letting a young man with glasses and a mustache tickle her most private parts!

The passionate grandmother had not asked to receive these telegraphic messages, but she was definitely receiving them. Her son, the child's father, was no help; he only told her she was being irrational. And her daughter-in-law—forget it! The passionate grandmother had once, nine years earlier, called her daughter-in-law a bad word, and that word had never been forgotten. The daughter-in-law carried the word around like an invisible helium balloon fastened to her wrist. The passionate grandmother sat there sniffing a fragrant yellow guest soap in the shape of a bunny, trying to calm her senses.

"When I'm done I want to show you something else," the child was saying to the blasé grandmother in the living room. The blasé grandmother sat solidly on her sofa, her hands folded in her lap, watching the powder room door and shaking her head. She wished for a cigarette, but she would have had to go outside to smoke it, a new rule made by the child's parents, even though it was the middle of winter, and what was one cigarette going to do to the child? On the other hand, knowing what was now known, she supposed that this was only being rational.

The blasé grandmother was the mother of the child's mother and was divorced. Not once but twice. She'd had her fill, she often declared these days. Her husbands were the least of her problems, really. She had come over on a boat from Hungary at the age of three, worked odd jobs for pay at the age of nine, and while raising her daughter, in between husbands, had never once paid for a single grocery item without using a coupon. Now, thanks to the divorces, she had plenty of money, not to mention a Senior Citizen card that made her eligible for fabulous bargains on almost everything. What was life for, if not to enjoy the nicer things? She owned so many floral-patterned silk scarves that she had lost count. She wore them draped and pinned artfully over her shoulders, and she enjoyed without guilt the sundry and not-so-sundry comforts and privileges now afforded her. She wanted the best for her grandchild, but she did not understand the problem. She personally had never flown off the handle in her life.

The passionate grandmother was the mother of the child's father and was widowed. Her husband had been a sober podiatrist who tried always to set aside his petty desires and work for the greater good, but in private he was a different kind of man, and she had enjoyed him terribly, at a time when this was considered unusual, even unnatural. They were especially fond of playing shocking practical jokes on each other at sacred moments, although many people who knew them well would have found this hard to believe. If anyone ever found out what she'd hidden in his can of foot powder on their honeymoon! She was a worrier even then, however, and when her son was a baby she bought for him a plastic amulet embossed with the message DON'T KISS ME in large ornate letters and strung on a white ribbon so it could hang enchantingly around his neck, protecting him from the germs of well-meaning strangers in public places. Then, after the baby was safely grown and away at college, her husband had one afternoon popped his handsome head up out of the crawl space and said, "I am a goblin of the deep," and she had laughed at him from the kitchen, where she was chopping carrots, and then he'd gone back down and had a cerebral hemorrhage and died.

Surprisingly, that event had not changed her personality much. During all those years she was enthusiastically loving her husband, she had in fact been living for her child—a guilty secret which had, she suspected, helped or even allowed her to love her husband. So, after grieving for him a while in public and a while longer in private, she went on living for her child, just as she always had, and when that was no longer realistic, she lived for her child's child. Why else did one live? she wondered. The child's fears were her own, and she would fight, if necessary, to keep from relinquishing them.

The child is scared of everything, the child's parents said. They recited this to strangers in department stores and waiting rooms and restaurants, even if the child was sitting quietly at that moment. It was impossible to take her anywhere, they said. They said it sometimes with scorn, other times irony, and still other times resignation. They took the child to a restaurant called the Ivanhoe that featured catacombs you descended to by elevator. The catacombs contained creative surprises especially for children, the nice lady who ran the elevator said. She had a sweet, apologetic voice and yellow hair in the shape of an optimistic, upward-floating bubble. Nevertheless, the child refused to go. Well, she got into the elevator but then caused such a scene the elevator had to be stopped and reversed. *Of course, what were we thinking?* the child's parents said. *She's scared of everything*, they told the nice lady. The lady worriedly worked the controls, her hair aquiver with concern. *And whatever she isn't scared of, she feels sorry for*, they told her.

Next door to the child lived an exceedingly large black dog. Half Great Dane, half Rottweiler, half *Clydesdale*, the dog's owner liked to say. He was a fat-cheeked personal injury attorney who advertised on the local TV channel. "An accident is just that—an accident," he said on his commercial. One would have thought the child would have been scared of the dog, but she wasn't. She was worried about the dog. The dog lived in a chain-link fenced enclosure that gave it plenty of room to run, but it didn't run much. It stood dead-still, right up next to the fence on the side of its enclosure that bordered the child's yard, its boulder-sized head pointed at the child's back door. If someone stepped outside, the dog began to tremble, and then, if the person took one more step toward the enclosure, the dog hurled it-self into the air, releasing a heartbreaking bark so loud and deep it was difficult to comprehend. The dog was lonely! The child visited the dog often, poking her fingers through the chain-link grid to pet the animal. The dog would turn sideways, shivering with desire, and when her fingers touched its side it would shut its eyes, a cracking noise seeming to come from deep within it. The child could not stand to hear the noise. And the fence drove her crazy—she could only squeeze four fingers through and then she could barely move her hand at all. The dog barked and shivered and hurled itself about, desperate for her, and she pushed her fingers through and moved them dutifully back and forth in a spot the size of a baseball card. The dog was so big, and she could touch so little of it!

Her parents gave each other knowing looks when they saw the child doing this. The child was going to ask for a dog. They were good parents and they could see it coming. They were better parents than a lot of parents. There was a boy in the child's second-grade class whose mother whipped him with a Hot Wheels race-track, for instance. It was common knowledge. And the three Logan children could be seen any Sunday morning picking Japanese beetles from the trees in their yard and dropping them into Chase & Sanborn coffee cans of gasoline, their father grimly supervising from behind the picture window, his arms folded. The child's parents would never do anything like that. When it was time, they would get the child a dog and the dog would teach the child valuable skills while helping her get over her fears.

Actually, though, the child didn't want a dog. What she wanted more than anything was an invisible-dog leash. The leash looked like a regular leash but extended magically out into the air by it-self and hung there as though an invisible dog were on it, the dog's neck filling out the open "O" of the collar. The leash was red, or at least all the ones the child had seen were red. The child asked for one for Christmas every year but she never got one. It was just plain stupid, her parents said, not even funny. It was not even clever.

She thought she could make one herself, maybe. She had a choice: Either find a way to make rope stiff or make something already stiff, such as a stick or pole, look like rope. Of course she had no rope, but her mother kept in the linen closet a skein of thick red yarn from which she cut lengths to tie off the child's pigtails. The child unwound the yarn and glued it to a yardstick, but the yardstick was too stiff and did not by any stretch of the imagination appear to hang, so she removed the yarn and coated it with Elmer's glue and lay it on the lawn to dry. But she hadn't bargained on the yarn just soaking up the glue the way it did. It just drank it up, like it was doing it on purpose. The child began to get irritated. The yarn was not getting stiff at all. It got soggy, then rubbery, then gray from her touching it, with grass blades stuck along its underside.

The big dog had watched her in its usual way when she first came outside, but after a while it went to sleep, lying flat with its big head resting on its front paws, still pointed right at her. She noticed this about the same time she gave up and sat back on her heels, surrounded by the horrid, ruined yarn. The dog went on sleeping, oblivious. Seeing this, she was angry, and then, a moment later, a little panicky.

• • •

The passionate grandmother had a secret. Obviously, she wasn't very good at keeping her feelings to herself, but there was one thing she had not revealed to anybody, had not allowed even herself to acknowledge. Well, she had acknowledged it, but she would not turn and greet it, for that would imply recognition. She knew once she recognized it she was done for. That was the kind of secret it was. It concerned her own demise, lying in wait for her, hidden somewhere in her future. It concerned the cause of her demise, harbored invisibly within her even now, somewhere deep within her body's connective tissue. She kept this secret not for her own sake but for the sake of the child.

"How old are you?" the child often asked her. The passionate grandmother was a little vain. Not a lot, but somewhat vain. *Oh, I was never what you would call beautiful*, she sometimes said, *but I knew how to walk into a room.*

"I'm as old as my tongue, and a little older than my teeth," she told the child.

The child loved this. "How old?" she would demand, leaping excitedly around in her grandmother's face.

But the passionate grandmother always said the same thing. The child usually kept on for a while and then eventually gave up. Then the two of them would sit smiling at each other in silence, each worried in her own way but still smiling at the other, at all that could not be understood about the other.

• • •

Christmas is coming and there is much discussion over what to get for the child. The child's parents discuss the issue in their bedroom with their door shut; the grandmothers discuss it in the Chevy Nova on their way to and from the child's house. The parents discuss it with the grandmothers on the telephone, abruptly falling silent when the child skips or sidles by. A puppy is not yet warranted, it is decided, so the child's father begins construction on a dollhouse in his utility room, trying to hammer softly after the child has gone to bed. He has everything he needs: clean blond sheets of pine, glass cut to fit the windows, carpet samples to lay on the floors. It will be a three-story townhouse with an attic, two staircases, and balconies with flower boxes and real wrought-iron railings. The child's father has never known quite what to make of the child's fears, but he sure knows how to make a dollhouse.

The child's mother shops for fabrics with unusual and whimsical designs to use for the dollhouse's curtains, bedspreads, towels, tablecloths, and wallpaper. She takes the child along on several of these excursions, her manner breezy and matter-of-fact as usual, and as usual the child prowls around the store by herself, returning to her mother's side only to beg her to hurry up so they can leave. The child's mother enjoys the deception. She will tell the child after the surprise, of course; that's half the fun. The child will demand to know on which shopping trip the fabric buying took place, and she will warn the child to pay closer attention in the future, not to be so trusting.

The child has asked again for an invisible-dog leash, and this year it looks like she might get one, from the blasé grandmother. "That sounds like a cute idea," the blasé grandmother says, when the child excitedly explains it to her. "See how long she likes it once she gets it," the child's mother says, but the blasé grandmother shrugs. The child is only a child, after all.

The passionate grandmother is the only one who can't figure out what to get. "She's made a list, I'll be happy to give you her list," the child's mother tells her, barely managing to conceal her exasperation. She has told the passionate grandmother this at least a half dozen times already.

"I believe in spontaneous gift-giving," the passionate grandmother says, not without exasperation herself. Whoever dreamed up lists?

"Well, you're on your own, then," the child's mother says. "I mean, your guess is as good as mine," she adds, feeling a little guilty. But that's ridiculous, why should she feel guilty? After what the woman once called her, right to her face . . .

The passionate grandmother lies awake at night, wondering. The question seems somehow more pressing than it was in past years. She has been thinking about it for months, actually since long before they started up with their lists, their secrets, their smirks and whispered conversations. Items pass before her open eyes in the dark—balls, board games, sweater sets, easels—all unacceptable. As if to compensate in advance for what will turn out to be an inadequate gift, she has begun telling the child certain things, truths, more or less. "The ugly is of course more compelling than the pretty," she tells her, for example, "although the pretty certainly enjoys its day." Another time she tells her: "Love is more reliable than many an actuality." Still another time she says, "Robert Dole is evil." She doesn't know where these statements come from; a context is never suggested. They simply arrive in her head, and so she speaks them.

The child, for her part, seems unfazed. She listens, stretching and unstretching her Chinese jump rope, asking questions as automatically as ever. "Only in loss can one find salvation," the passionate grandmother tells her, and the child asks what salvation is. The passionate grandmother suddenly recalls the days right after her husband's death, the strange, hollow days with her own child nearly grown, but before this child. This child sits Indian-style, waiting for her answer, hugging herself—but her little freckled arms are so skinny, the passionate grandmother notes with alarm, so frail-looking, so inadequate to the task! She has to turn away.

The father comes home early from work one afternoon a few days before Christmas to put the last touches on the doll-house, and the mother takes the child to see a behavior specialist to get her out of the way. The specialist is a kind-faced, rather sloppy man named Dr. Boonstra. His shirts are always stained in odd places, his nose shiny as a teenager's, but he comes recommended by the child's elementary school. He has met several times already with the child and the child's parents, though it remains to be seen whether he will have any success in exterminating the child's fears. And why *can't* it be as simple as calling the exterminator? the child's mother wonders.

This time Dr. Boonstra talks with the child alone. He ushers her into his warm, messy office and shows her a series of pictures, realistic black line drawings on white cardboard cards. Each drawing represents a familiar object, Dr. Boonstra explains, something the child might expect to see around the house every day, such as a toaster or a bicycle or a turtleneck sweater. But each object is missing one of its parts, a crucial part, and it will be the child's task to figure out what. The bicycle, for instance, is missing its handlebars. Does the child understand? What is missing is more important than what is there. Dr. Boonstra leans forward, resting his elbows on his knees so that his hands will be steady holding the cards before the child's eyes.

The child proceeds eagerly through the stack, feeling satisfaction each time she correctly identifies what is absent. She is successful with the lamp, bucket, rolling pin, and TV set, but she gets stuck on the scissors. She cannot find anything missing from the scissors. The second blade? No, the scissors are closed. The screw? No, the screw is right there. Another screw? No, there is only one screw. "Nothing's missing!" the child guesses—it's a trick! But no, something is definitely missing, Dr. Boonstra says.

She looks more closely at the picture, Dr. Boonstra tilting it helpfully toward the light. "The paper?" she asks. No, there is no paper, only the scissors. "The screw?" she asks again, weakly. Dr. Boonstra's face is friendly but serious. She has all the time in the world. She puts her face right up next to the card and stares as hard as she can, gritting her teeth and holding her breath, as though if she can just focus hard enough she will be able to see what is invisible. "*Nothing's* missing!" she blurts out, finally. She is getting angry. *What is missing is more important than what is there*, Dr. Boonstra reminds her. She goes on making the same guesses over and over, until finally she is bored. She doesn't care anymore, she is positive nothing is missing. Dr. Boonstra never does tell her the correct answer.

"What did you do today?" the child's mother asks him, writing out his check at the end of the hour.

Dr. Boonstra is famously vague. "Oh, a little of this, a little of that," he says. The child's mother is not thrilled about these responses but she understands the notion of professionalism, at least. Dr. Boonstra nods as politely as he can at the mother and notes that the child appears slightly fiercer than she was last week. And last week slightly more so than the week before. *Everything in its time*, he thinks. "Take her home and love her!" he calls after them in the parking lot, waving at the child, who waves back.

"You know what my mother would call a man like that?" the child's mother says, reaching over the front seat to make sure the child's belt is fastened safely. "Tooty-fruity." The child giggles, imagining the blasé grandmother saying this. The child's mother laughs with her, and they drive along like that, giggling together from their places in the front and back seats.

That night, in the middle of the night, the passionate grandmother awakens. It is not yet Christmas, but almost. She still hasn't found a gift for the child, but that isn't what woke her, not this time. It was something else. Something has changed. She thought she heard music, but there is no music. She was having a dream, maybe that's what it was. Her little bedroom is quiet and blue-gray, as usual, her sheets still tucked neatly into the corners of her little twin bed, holding her snugly in place. But something has changed. She lies there warily, trying to remember her dream.

What comes to mind instead is her son, who as a child always awoke from his dreams bewildered or heartbroken. "There's a canoe in my bed!" he'd exclaimed to her one time, nearly weeping with excitement. "Oh, where are you going?" she had asked, keeping her voice casual. He seemed taken aback by this, and after a moment he told her he didn't know. "Well, are you happy?" she asked him gently. "Yes," he'd said, and then he looked relieved, and she herself had nearly wept with relief, tucking him back in. And what was it her husband always said, when she returned to their bed? He had not approved. *You are not making it any better for him, always being there*, he would say. What do you know about it? she would argue, and he would roll over to his side of the bed, saying, *Fine, have it your way, but only in your absence will he learn.* Only in your absence . . .

The child! The dream that woke her crashes, almost audibly, back into her brain. The child was there, tied to her wrist with some kind of yellow string, but the knots were poorly tied and the child came loose, suddenly floating upward and away from her against a clear white sky. She had no time, no chance to stop it, the child was already too far up, looking back down at her with a puzzled expression. *Grandmother?* the child called uncertainly. She was not yet panicked, only confused. The grandmother tried to yell but no sound came, and when she tried to leap after the child, the weight of what must have been the whole earth held her down. Her heart beat like a bird against a window. *Grandmother?* the child called, but her thin voice was moving steadily away, getting harder and harder to hear, her body growing impossibly small against the giant sky. *Can you hear me? Grandmother?*

She lies in bed, her hand on her heart. The child is fine, the child is safe, she is not in the sky, she's at home. She is in her bedroom, tidying up, the grandmother can see her now.

She understands now what has changed. And it is odd, incidentally, very odd, for she has always assumed, like most people, that it is the dead who float off toward the sky, the living who remain below. For this is what has changed: Her secret has arrived. It will be a secret no longer.

The idea that she should be frightened registers like a speck of dust on a distant backdrop, then vanishes. She shuts her eyes and focuses on the child, whom she can see as clearly as if it were full daylight. The child is in her room, on the floor, kneeling over something on the yellow carpet and concentrating hard, her hair making a shiny curtain that covers her eyes on both sides, like blinders. Around her the room is tidy, the pine toy-chest closed, the polka-dotted comforter covering the bed, the mismatched stuffed animals set up in a neat half-circle on a shelf. The child has learned from her grandmothers the importance of taking care of one's belongings, the necessity of surrounding one's self with beautiful things. The child crouches now, engrossed in some scrap of paper or bit of cloth, oblivious. But around her, everything is in place, everything is exactly as it will need to be.

success story

Claire from upstairs had a brother who from the time he was little would go outside and come back in with snakes, snakes nobody even saw until he casually picked them out of the grass and offered them for your view. This was something Claire told me, and after she told me I could not seem to hear or see enough of him. He and Claire were tall, handsome interns at a stable, both of them chattering about bots and mash and foundering hooves, sharing blue jeans so that sometimes when I saw a pair of strong faded legs striding by my basement window my stomach would clench up and then it would turn out to be silly Claire, leaving me embarrassed. I tried to get them in for coffee, and spent time sitting in each of my chairs, gauging Claire's brother's view of my narrow rooms, my parents' hand-me-down bridge tables and cheap ethnic hangings. But only Claire ever came, squinting and dusty after work, carrying her velvet-wrapped huntcap, which she kept on her lap the whole time. She told me about her day indiscriminately and I had to wait, blank-faced, for the topic of her brother to come up, feeling real pain somewhere behind my ribs. He wore two button-down flannel shirts on cold mornings, one under the other, his blond chest under them, and seeing this from my window, or imagining it later while I pretended to listen to Claire, gave me angry waves and chills, hard frustration.

Claire was all right, though, in that she never caught on, or pretended not to catch on, and spoke in great swells of over-statement, sometimes making me pay attention to her in spite of myself. "I fixed that trunk lock a hundred and fifty thousand times yesterday," she'd say, or "That sick horse has more worms than veins." Then she would laugh, surprised at herself, and I'd laugh, and she'd say, "Why don't you come down there with us, Caroline, and we'll take you out on the trail? It's free, with us, you know."

"I know," I said. "It's not the money." I always left it at that, wanting to go, but not wanting to be seen as a novice; surely I would get up on the wrong side of the horse, or call the horse the wrong thing, or steer the horse into a wall, or make other equestrian mistakes that I was too inexperienced to even imagine.

Claire tried; she told me riding was all predilection and magic, that she and Dale only did it because when they were teenagers they'd gotten stuck with an ugly pony their grandfather left them in his will. They'd tried raffling the pony off to the neighborhood kids, but the ticket Dale drew had their own names on it, mysteriously, and that was that, here they were making a career of it. "Besides, you can't just sit in here a million hours a day," she said. "Don't you just want to shoot out the ceiling?"

"I think I have the ideal situation," I said. In the corner were twelve cartons of the makings of brochures, which I sorted and assembled and once a week drove to a warehouse downtown, where I was given more cartons, as many as I could fit in my car. I was one of the people who made direct-mail advertising work for *me*, said the caption under my picture in the newspaper ad that ran continuously. I was a success story, and my smiling face seduced dozens of lazy others into signing up. But I'd been doing it the longest.

"Never drive on a slant street," my mother always said, meaning: Don't do what you don't know how to do. I followed this and thought it was better to *imagine* Dale taking my sweater from my shoulders, imagine him learning that my bra unhooked in front, than it was to go ahead and accept Claire's invitation and make a fool of myself at the stables.

Once when I went up to their apartment I saw something small and curved glinting on a dresser in their back room and thought it must be Dale's—part of a knife or razor—but it turned out to be Claire's barrette, and this made me wonder: was petty danger all I wanted? I noticed messy tins of polish and liniment on their kitchen counter, and week-old mail lying unopened on their bathroom floor, whereas at my place I knew which drawer my birth certificate was in, original and copy, and where I had a screwdriver small enough to repair the hinge on a pair of glasses, though I did not wear glasses. Tucked away in my bathroom closet were fresh tubes of toothpaste and sealed bottles of sinus tablets, of which, it was beginning to occur to me, I should be ashamed. So I went upstairs and sat on the fold-out sofa—where he slept—and got what I could from Claire, but it was never enough.

In February, when they'd been living upstairs for six months and the early morning swampiness in the air was almost unbearably sweet, I finally broke down about the stables, and then only because it was an emergency. Dale was at my door, suddenly, in a bright absurd slam of unexpectedness, telling me his truck had a bad clutch and would I mind? I put on my hard-soled shoes, the picture of straight-faced concern, and noted my comb and blusher on the dresser, unused and useless, and he bent idly to look at my one nice print. It was a Hondecoeter poster from an art museum, a somber group of birds exploding around a fallen crow, an allegory. "I've seen this," Dale said, improbable in his cowboy boots. "A Dutch guy?"

"Right," I said. "He was the one who knew how to paint birds."

"Oh, good, good, Caroline's finally going to ride," Claire said from the open doorway. We swept out, Dale leaving, I hoped, a shed hair or fingerprint or dried mud crumbling from his boot—in this way I might as well have been fifteen. I had once saved two curled hairs from the chest of a man I loved, storing them like contact lenses in an envelope, as if I could save enough to build another, more controllable him. It wasn't that I was superstitious, though, having had enough people love me or stop loving me for the wrong reason or for no reason—I was just starved for small encroachments on my small successful life.

• • •

The stable was set back from the highway by a yard of mud and gravel, overhung with Spanish moss that a few tied, waiting horses were chewing. Their stretched necks were clean and reflected my Chevy's headlights, but they didn't pause or look, though with their eyes in the sides of their heads I thought they might be taking us in. I had been on a horse once at camp or a carnival, and remembered only the stupid, clumsy way its neck looked from above, not storybook graceful or powerful in the least but more like a dead branch on a tree. "Don't even look at those duds," Claire said. "We ride the privately owned ones, who haven't been ridden by eight hundred brats a day until they can't even feel their own tongues in their mouths."

Dale, in my rearview mirror, had his head bent, and was fixing or playing with a button on his flannel shirt cuff. "That's right," he said. I saw his deliberate fingers on his cuff, on my sweater. I cut the engine, thinking: *snakes.*

The smell of the place was perfect, Dale a hundred times over: sawdust, leather, sweat, mildew, coffee, cedar. Three women even prettier and happier-looking than Claire stood in skin-tight breeches in the stable's office, drinking machine coffee out of paper cups and teasing a runny-eyed cat with their whips. "Connie, Rachel, Lynn," Dale said, nodding and leading us through. *He can't love all of them*, I thought.

"Look out," Claire said behind me, and we stepped around another cat who had a mouse or vole opened up on the concrete. Another memory came to me: a drunken man approaching me on my parents' front lawn and offering ten dollars and the end of a fifth of tequila if I gave him our Dalmatian. I wanted the money and the dog was boring, but I was afraid of being found out and of the tequila and so said no. This seemed an embarrassing corollary to Claire's raffle story, saying something about people who knew when to take a hint from their lives versus those who wouldn't, and I kept it to myself. Dale took us down aisles of cramped lead-in stalls, past dozens of horses' calm rumps, under ceilings of ropy cobwebs. In the back the stable opened up into airy box stalls for the boarder horses of higher quality.

"How about if she takes Cocktail Hour?" Claire said, and Dale nodded and unbolted the sliding door on one of the boxes, making the hefty chestnut inside sidestep and toss its head.

"It's nice that you get to ride these horses," I said, balking.

"We don't *get* to," Dale said, all the time working the heavy door, buckling a halter, chaining the big horse up for me. "That's what the boarders pay for—boarding, training, and exercise. We're training and exercise. Now we're going to make this easy for you, give you the *western* saddle, and just a snaffle . . ."

"Go on in," Claire said. "He won't breathe *fire* on you."

I stepped in and my feet sank a little, sawdust after concrete. Between Dale and me was the high red wall of the horse, not yet saddled. "This is the curry," Dale said, handing me something over the horse's shoulders. I knew something was about to happen as I reached for it, seeing the horse's muscles seem to contract under its skin. The sawdust shifted and I saw the chestnut's big head cocked like a kitten's, its white eye rolled back at me. I felt the wall of the horse's ribs against my ribs, my back hitting hard wood, and I thought: *Dale's ribs, I'm wearing the black bra,* and then I fainted.

• • •

"What will you do, what will you do?" I thought I heard someone saying, but when I really came to, Claire was saying, "Dad's gone genealogy insane," and Dale was holding a cold can of beer against my throat, and the way I was propped between them made me feel like some kind of king. "She's fine," Dale said, his fingers on my ribs.

"Caroline," Claire said, "did you know our great-great-grandfather was master of the hunt in England—I was just telling Dale that some people don't have horses in their blood like we do, *you* probably have sea blood or mine blood or wheat-field blood . . ."

"Shut up," Dale said.

I reached for the beer can at my neck, but he took it away, drank it off, crumpled it, and tossed it a few yards, all the time keeping his eyes on my face, his hand under my sweater. "Say something," he said, beginning to smile.

Something twitched under his hand, under my skin. "Oh," I said.

• • •

In college I once went tubing with my friends, a group of hopeful, sloppy-hearted girls like Claire. We went to the local cold springs the day before we all were to graduate, and for once I was relaxed enough not to talk or even paddle; we'd gotten through college, after all, so I lay back and shut my eyes against the Southern sun, altogether thrilled with such a batch of luck: friends, weather, success. What got me then was nothing as drastic as a cloudburst, but when I opened my eyes my friends had drifted a good thirty yards ahead, keeping hands on each other's tubes, and one of them was getting up on her knees, cheered by the others—I was at that moment invisible, and not just to them. Almost as an experiment after that I let things and people drift as far as they wanted, and found it didn't take anything away from my success. But now I was finding out the experiment's inverse: when someone drifted my way it was a windfall, it was winning the lottery. In all my wanting Dale, I had never thought so far as to *expect* him. In my small bedroom, finally, where he stayed when he came down to check on me the evening of my faint, he was as large and unlikely as a grand piano, a gift from another, richer world.

Claire came down inscrutably the next morning, carrying sweet rolls, and I couldn't tell if she was spying, consoling, or just visiting. Her knock gave me a small fit of remembering: Dale flexing his wrists like a weight lifter just before he took my face in his hands to kiss me; the lazy, satisfied way he stepped from my shower stall, male pride itself. "Don't give me any more coffee," Claire said. "My heart's about to explode. I just stopped in to ask a favor for Dale."

Favor, I thought, means she probably doesn't know, whatever *that* means. There were going to be rules now, and I was sure I didn't know them.

"Needs you to drive him to pick up his truck, if you're feeling up to it," she said.

"Oh, fine, fine," I said.

"Well," she said. She was in no hurry. She bent her long legs and sat in my armchair. I tried to think of what to say.

"So, do horses ever bite you?" I said.

"That ugly pony we had bit a baby," she said. "But that was because he knew we were trying to get rid of him. Or maybe the baby told him something terrible, I don't know. I do believe animals sense things, though. You know how they lie down on the ground when an earthquake is coming? I have a book about it. There was a chrysanthemum that could start a car! You can borrow that book if you want. Do you have a boyfriend?"

I had been wondering if she was trying to tell me in a veiled way that the chestnut had crushed me on purpose, perhaps for wanting Dale, for being a coward, or for something worse which only she and the horse were sensitive enough to see.

"I'm sorry," Claire said. She looked sorry. She divided a Danish the size of her face into two parts and offered me one. "I don't mean to give you a hard time," she said, "but I think he likes you. He may ask you out. He's been very touchy. The last time he liked someone he punched me."

"He punched you?" I repeated.

"I told him his sweetheart Gabrielle was a spoiled brat," she said. "She was born without sweat glands. She was a big star on the horse show circuit and her mother followed her around with ice packs all the time. All I said was that he could do a lot better."

"Was she pretty?" I said. I was encouraged, thinking that with her birth defect she couldn't have been beautiful, at least not hopelessly so. The punching still loomed, but it was secondary. "Could you tell what was wrong with her?"

"Well, she was thin, but that could have been anything," Claire said. "And then her eyes looked wrong, like her lids were inside out, and then she had scaly arms and scaly patches on her face."

"Actual scales?" I said.

"Hey, maybe that's why he was so crazy for her," Claire said. "Like a snake—ha!" We both laughed, but I thought she herself looked like a snake—a happy snake, with her wide, pretty mouth, her eyes narrowed against the morning sun. I told her I found it hard to believe Dale would punch her.

"Well, he didn't actually hit me," she said. "But he wanted to, I could see it. He was right up in my face. I said, 'Dale, what difference does my opinion make?' He said, 'You just don't understand her. You don't understand anyone who hasn't had it easy.' I said, 'Dale, tell me one thing that hasn't come easy for you. Name one thing.'" She stopped there and shook her head. I waited to hear Dale's answer, but she just sat there in the light, chewing her

Danish, giving away nothing. When she left my place, she warned me that he might ask me "for a date," and she spoke to my Hondecoeter with what could only be innocence. She touched her finger to the fallen crow as if it were some cute calendar puppy. "Bye, birdies," she said.

That same day I had to take my cartons in to the warehouse, and the traffic and scenery on the way were suddenly extraordinary, unpredictable. I passed what I thought was a bearded lady at a bus stop, but when I did a doubletake it turned out to be an Amish man. Then, at the warehouse, after I'd done my business and loaded my car, I caught myself getting in through my *passenger* door, as if I were my own guest. The snakes were what I kept thinking about, because I hadn't managed to ask him about them. We had, in fact, barely spoken—I remembered him saying only my name into my shoulder—and I hadn't wanted to ruin it with questions. Now, though, I was already longing for something else from him, wanting to see bearded ladies the way he saw snakes, wanting to know more than I knew. I didn't want to sit around forever with an envelope full of chest hairs.

I was expecting a phone call when it was time for me to go to the stables, but instead an angry-looking wrecker driver knocked on my windowpane, catching me doing nothing, lying with my head on a stack of incorrectly assembled brochures. I met him on the lawn, blushing, and said, "I don't understand."

"Nothing to worry about, miss," he said. We were eye to eye, the same height, only his legs seemed to start much lower than mine—he stood anchored and dungareed, a step too close to me. "As *I* understand it," he said, "Dale didn't want you to put yourself out, since we take him out to the garage anyway. Since I was on a call in your neighborhood, our dispatch said to swing around for you, as a favor, and you'll meet him at the garage." He spoke reasonably, but he really did appear to be furious about something, so I didn't ask questions.

His double-parked truck was not a glorified pickup but the big kind, the back of it loaded with mean-looking wheels and cogs and cables; stepping up into it was like getting on The Spider or The Crazy Zipper at a fair. Inside were empty apple-juice cans, dirty socks and sweatshirts, a tuna smell, and short white hairs stuck to the velour seats—it looked like small children lived there. "Don't mind the mess," he said.

"I won't," I said.

"I mean I don't," he said.

We roared off down the highway that led out of town, passing the stables and everything else I was familiar with, and hit a stretch of neatly spaced longleaf pines that went on indefinitely on both sides of the road. It seemed impolite to ask how far away the garage was.

"What are you, an artist?" the driver said. He was looking sideways at my ripped T-shirt, my ink-spotted jeans.

"No, I'm in direct-mail advertising for a number of different firms," I said.

"Oh, I know all about that," he said. "You ever go to conventions? We hit 'em all the time, believe it or not. Tow-truck conventions. I was up in Chicago just last month, in fact. Got a ticket for doing eighty on the Dan Ryan."

The pines whipped by more rapidly and the pile of socks under my feet seemed to expand and shift, which I took to be another hallucination. The driver's stubbly face, lit through the windshield, was scornful. "Those boys up there," he said, shaking his head, "they stopped me and told me I was driving like I wanted to kill someone. 'You'll get yourself killed,' they told me, but I said, *Nope, I can't be kilt.*"

Something that I thought might be a rolled sock nudged my ankle—it was a kitten, the source of the white hairs. The kitten and I both cried out at the same moment, making the driver turn his head. "Can't train that thing to save my life," he said.

The kitten fawned and slithered absurdly around my legs. "Can you train cats?" I said, a little angry, wondering if the kitten got any water or anything decent to eat.

"No, that's what I'm *saying*," said the driver, sounding even angrier. We sat in silence for a couple of minutes. "They should have someone like that English *dog* lady, only for these damned cats," he grumbled, and we fell into more angry silence, me watching the kitten, the driver not looking my way again. Finally he said, "Well, we're almost there, you might as well sit back and enjoy the rest of the duration."

There was something bothering me, something I wanted to ask Dale, and I wanted to hear his side on the sweat gland girl—but when we pulled up to the garage, the sight of his broad back blotted everything out. He was in the driveway, relaxing against his truck and talking to a couple of garage men, the group of them shaded by a row of young pines. Behind the building tall thick trees went back in levels, with no gaps for houses or roads or electrical lines. The men, including Dale, all stood like the tow-truck driver: casual, anchored. I thought how attractive scorn could be, and took some reassurance in the way they all stood—Dale might not be the only source of what I wanted. "Thanks for the lift," I told the driver. He nodded and spat on the ground.

"Sweetheart," Dale said, and held out his arm, and I was helpless again, so close to his unshaven cheek. The other men lowered their eyes politely. "You look happy," he said. "You been hanging around my sister?"

In his truck I stopped comparing him to the garage driver and compared him to Claire, whose light eyes and airy profile he shared. From the side, you could actually see through their irises, but you couldn't tell a thing from looking at either one of them. I imagined any of the pretty stable girls would have given him a ride. "Where are we going?" I said.

We were heading deeper into the layers of trees, which turned out to have a gravel road cutting through them after all. Rocks and acorns popped under us, startling me, and the damp afternoon heat buzzed in through the cabin's open windows. I waited, sweating and vibrating. It was beginning to hurt to take deep breaths.

"You ever hear about the poisoned oak?" Dale said.

"Poison oak?" I said.

"No, that old live oak some loony tried to kill. It was in the paper, maybe you missed it."

I had heard about it. People from town had come out with candles and coins, statues of Mary, and cans of soup, which they placed on the ground among the sick tree's knotty roots. The oak recovered, and the poisoner was nabbed in his trailer. The poison would be what Dale liked, I thought. "It's something to see," he said. "Big old thing. I figured you hadn't been out to it yet." I glanced at him, expecting scorn, but he looked perfectly involved, perfectly thrilled, steering us over the pitted road with a sure hand.

He cut the engine in what was barely a clearing, and the sudden silence hurt my ears. From where we were, the low trunk-sized branches of the oak were visible, running along horizontally in the light shade of the younger trees. The trunk itself was farther back, lurking like a great black bear in the brush. Dale jumped out and slammed his door, already gazing at something off beyond the tree. "What is it?" I said, but he didn't answer. He saw whatever it was he saw, liked what he liked, leaving me to sit there on the creaky truck seat in my own aching, breathing separateness. This may have been selfishness on his part, but it was not deliberate, not tricky, and there was no getting around its appeal. A tiresome wave of my own scheming energy washed back on me. He was right. Where we were was beautiful, and no place I would have driven on my own. I climbed down and went to look at the recovering tree.

• • •

I remembered what I wanted to ask, finally, when we were in bed that night. We were flat on our backs, not touching, staring up into the sweet, swampy dark and listening to Claire's quick footsteps on their linoleum. Breathing still hurt, but being smashed by the horse seemed old and doubtful already. "About the snakes," I said, "that you used to find?"

"I can still find 'em," Dale said. "Got an eye."

"How?" I said. "Or I mean why?"

"It's just something I know how to do," he said. "What boy doesn't like snakes? Well, you don't have a brother."

I considered the dangerous curve of him. What was it about his sure, unquestioning self that went into me like grappling hooks? Even in the heart of fulfilled longing was this anger in me for more, more than him even.

"You can still find snakes?" I said, not caring but needing to talk.

"Hell, honey," he said, "I can show you that, but that's not the most exciting thing about me."

He moved onto me again, and the last thing I thought of was the time I watched that English dog-trainer's show and saw a tense line of dog owners backing on tiptoe away from a corresponding line of dogs, who were being taught to *stay*. The people moved silently, their arms outstretched in the *stay* command, and the dogs seemed unconcerned, and the widening space between them was miraculous, thick with hope. I saw myself like the tiptoeing dog owners, silently retreating from everything that was too easy about my life, hoping nothing would break the spell.

easy

I'm not even out of Florida and already thinking of my mother:
the sun-bleached billboard for House of Porcelain reminds me
of the ceramics she took up after my father died. She called it
"mastering an art," and she did it so that when she looked at me
she would not be so distracted by his eyes, his chin; she wanted
to make the hard first months easier. She set up shop on our
screened porch, replacing my father's shelves of hardware with
ten-pound bags of wet clay and a kiln she assembled from a kit,
and soon the porch filled up with coy-faced rabbits and round-
limbed, winking frogs. She glazed them conservatively in calm
opaques and garnished each with a set of stick-on eyelashes,
which she thought was a cute idea and I thought made the animals appear hopeful. When one fell and smashed, with those
eyelashes, it was heartbreaking.

She could probably cut a deal with the House of Porcelain
people—their billboards boast of "spirited porcelain children"

and "fragile crystal relics from a simpler time"—but I can't afford to stop and browse. My plan is not to get off the highway until I'm in Georgia, which is not just superstition, though Georgia sounds safe to me with all its bragging about such harmless commodities as peaches and pecans. By the time I reach Georgia, I've figured, my mother should be up and eating her Danish, and I can phone her from some anonymous reststop and tell her I'm on my way. Like an athlete, I visualize my successful arrival, picture her spare house key, which sits in the mouth of a ceramic squirrel that's frozen in an adorable crouch and nailed to the front steps of her Chicago house. She sculpted the squirrel herself, using neither mold nor model. I picture the highway stretching out ahead of me, the squirrel at one end and me, a dot, at the other, like a puzzle in a children's magazine. But there on my left thigh is a quarter-sized blue bruise from Charlie, and it too is the dot. I whip along, going seventy, my hand resting lightly on the bruise, which also goes seventy.

• • •

There was a time, just after my father's death, that my mother would never have let me get this far out of her sight. I was just starting first grade, so she took a job serving food in my school cafeteria. She may have been possessive, even compulsive, but I loved that it was my own mother's hand placing the extra cookies on my tray. Lunch was like a daily personal gift, somehow connected to my father, whom I couldn't exactly remember. I knew that she was there *for* me, but *because* of him, and I sometimes wondered if he had actually told her to give me the cookies. She stayed on for eight years, and because she was younger than the rest of the cafeteria staff and served with a mild, surprised look on her face, while the other women scowled and had drawn-on eyebrows, my mother was popular. She knew every kid's name and she made jokes about the food she served. She could afford to; she had chosen to be there.

When I went off to high school we thought our arrangement had ended: the high school cafeteria workers had a union and wouldn't even accept my mother's application. But then she found out the company that serviced the school's vending machines was hiring, so she became the new candy bar lady. Now only the greasers joked with her, the guys in navy tanker jackets who hung out by her machines talking about Auto Mechanics Lab and looking too old to be in high school. They were shiny-faced, actually greasy, and often red-eyed, and they clomped around the halls in black lace-up boots, jingling large bunches of keys that were attached to their belts with heavy link chains. Their girlfriends looked cleaner but wore clunky wooden sandals that made as much noise as the boys' boots and keys, and they went around with giant combs sticking out of their back pockets. They all looked shrewd and unhappy, as though they expected to hear bad news at any moment, and my mother would tell me stories. "Kimmy Forsythe is not as dumb as she looks," she would say to me at home. "She is the sole guardian of her four little brothers, not one but *two* of whom are diagnosed hyperactive." Or she might say, "You should be nice to the Mazzetti boys. They don't even hear how they sound to others, and they have a terrible time of it at home." By now I felt I was indulging my mother, that her job was a way of ensuring that *she* was okay. One of us needed to feel that one of us was safe, but the roles had grown hazy, as roles will do.

Occasionally some guy I'd never spoken a word to would bump into me in one of my classes and say, "You got a nice ma." This always embarrassed me—I had it easier than the Mazzetti boys and I knew it. I wasn't jealous of my mother's attentions to them, and I didn't secretly want to run away with them, or marry them, or be them. My friends and I ignored the greasers and laughed a little at their girlfriends' clothes, but mostly we did our homework and went to movies and our boring jobs. I was a weekend hatcheck girl at a Holiday Inn and was already thinking of going on in art, not for the rebellion or the romance, but because of how simple my mother made ceramics look. I was never one to look for trouble.

• • •

I remind myself of this as I pull off of I-75, finally, safely into Georgia, at a stop called Arabi, which I know only because it's written on the rusted pay phone in front of the gas station. Beyond the station there's just an empty road curving away into the high tree line. "I'm coming home," I tell my mother. "I'm on my way right now."

"That's odd," she says. "I mean, not strange that you're coming, but Charlie just telephoned for you here." She and Charlie have never met, but they know each other's phone voices.

"I didn't tell him I was leaving," I say. "He's the reason I'm coming."

My mother doesn't say anything for a moment. Finally she says, "Well, I told him I didn't know anything about where you were, since of course I didn't. What time will you be here?"

"Late," I say. "Or in the morning."

"Wake me up if you want," she says.

I fix my hair for a minute in the silver reflection on the phone's coin box before walking over to the little cinder-block building to pay for my gas. Inside, a large man with a face the color and texture of stone sits behind the counter, watching a newscast on a black-and-white wall television. He nods and takes my money. On the TV a man is speaking in Chinese, and a translation appears beneath him: "We couldn't determine whether here is a detective."

"They're everywhere," the man says to me, sliding me my change. "When you least expect it, expect it." He might be talking about detectives, communists, the Chinese—it's impossible to tell. "You traveling alone?" he says.

"Not far," I lie.

"Be careful, that's all I'm saying," he says. I thank him and back out, keeping my eyes on a spot on his shirt.

Georgia is a lengthy drive, south to north, and it keeps getting foggier and hillier. I listen to all-talk radio and learn unlikely things, that "alfalfa" is Arabic for "father of all foods," that racehorses aren't allowed more than seventeen letters in their names, and that in Tokyo lonely old people rent actors to play visiting sons and daughters, actors who are trained how to laugh and how to say goodbye. These all seem like fine things to know for now—if nothing else, they are things I didn't know while I was with Charlie. They make as much sense as anything. Life, I think, is like one of those games where everyone sits in a circle and each person must, in turn, remember one more item in a series. You have to remember the whole series each time, in order, or else you are out.

Early this morning I tiptoed out of the bedroom, my smallest muscles tensed. But Charlie didn't wake up; his face remained puffy and unmenacing in sleep. I went out to my car, expecting determent: slashed tires, a dead battery, anything. I remembered once when I was a child and my mother had planned a driving trip, packing up the car the night before, as I had now. In the morning when she opened the driver's side door, a kinglet flew out—the tiniest, most perfect bird I'd ever seen. This morning, now that I was finally leaving, I expected and even hoped for something like that to happen, but there was nothing to stop me, to make me think. The best I could come up with was the raspberry Danish someone had splattered all over my windshield a few days earlier, when I'd been withdrawing my savings from the bank. I hadn't taken it personally, because the parking lot was crowded and I was inside for half an hour, but when I mentioned it to Charlie, leaving out the part about my savings, of course, he said a woman had probably done it. He said a man wouldn't mess with something as petty as a sweet roll. "A man would've bent your rearview or broken off your antenna," he said.

I told him he was wrong, that women had respect for things like Danishes, and men didn't. He just laughed, the way he kept me from ever being right about anything. I remember still thinking stubbornly: A woman wouldn't do that to a Danish.

What I can't remember is when I got used to being wrong so often. It started with such minor things—what kind of dish drainer we should own, whether to keep his clock radio or mine by the bed, which was the superior brand of corn flakes. I had no experience with bullies. We'd met at someone's back-yard party by a kudzu-covered wall where I'd chosen to drink, and his awful confidence had probably only seemed whole-some, as solid and natural a part of my happy evening as the beautiful green-and-rock wall. I don't even remember when we began to speak, or what was said. It didn't seem like an event, which was probably why I trusted it. I knew if something seemed too good to be true, it probably was, and I put no stock in Princes Charming. My life was solitary and easy then. I was stagnating happily in a futureless position as a keyliner for a commercial line of do-it-yourself books, walking home from work each night with bits of sentences and diagrams stuck in my hair. I still grinned at geckos and cypress trees, even though I'd lived in the South for the three years since college and those things should have been routine. I would sit and watch my lionhead goldfish for ninety minutes at a stretch, talking out loud to him and feeling every bit as satisfied as I would if he had understood me. I had peace and I trusted in it.

Charlie, at first, seemed to fit into my life so easily; he kissed me like it was just another way of breathing. He hugged me tightly and with purpose, the way you hold a child who's just come home from summer camp. We would be kissing and I would open my eyes and his would already be open, as if he were waiting for me. He worked in a distant and glamorous de-partment of my company, in public relations, and when he spoke about us, he spoke with great confidence. He spoke as if it were only a matter of time before most people agreed with him about most things. He laughed at hesitation and uncertainty in any form, and when he talked he made small, finalizing gestures with his large hands. I had been content with the banal—my fish, the Spanish moss, an occasional barbecue—but Charlie brought need, strong desire, and he did it with elegance, with grand finesse. "How this turns out," he said frequently in his salesman's voice, "is up to you." "Whatever you want," a phrase of indulgence, became, over time, imbued with menace. I wasn't sure *what* I wanted, having never wanted much. Now, the more I wanted him, the more inevitable, immutable we seemed. It wasn't long before I couldn't remember ever *not* wanting him, ever being happy without him. Why was I arguing with him, why was I making myself so unhappy?

On one Sunday morning, the morning after the first really bad time, we sat side by side like peaceful grandparents on the sunny second-floor landing outside our apartment's back door. I kept getting distracted by the faint humid wind blowing beneath my legs and by my sore scalp, which felt in the sun as though it were heating from within. My whole body felt hungover, though we had not been drunk. Sitting between us on the concrete, like some Martian child, was a small roll-on bottle of Absorbine Jr. which Charlie had gotten from the 7-Eleven after breakfast, when I'd complained. He'd been silent, dabbing the cool medicine on my bare back and arms, the sore places from the night before where he had yanked me or where I'd pulled too hard to get away, and now the sweet minty smell steamed up from me, both foreign and reassuring. I hung onto the smell as though it really were a child, or a gift, as though it were the first thing about us.

The day wobbled along around us, the fight of the night before looming everywhere and yet seeming unreal, comic, impossible to apprehend, like the balls and blobs of mercury from a broken thermometer, shaken from their context—dangerous, but in a way you could neither believe in nor ignore. We said little, both of us apparently wanting his apologies behind us. I had forgiven him hurriedly, feeling while doing it a rush of instinctive relief not unlike getting my head above water after a long submersion. That anything else lay down there still, beneath my relief, was not a possibility I considered.

After a while a neighbor's cat trotted by, carrying in its mouth a women's pink cardigan sweater, as though this were a sensible thing for it to be doing. A short unnatural laugh came out of me, and the cat's eyes shifted my way for an instant, then back at the sidewalk, the cat itself never breaking stride, the sweater sleeves swinging on either side of its stuffed jaws. I put my sore head down and laughed, great gulping laughs like gasping for breath. "You see?" I heard Charlie say. "That's what I mean."

"What are you talking about?" I said. I didn't sit up.

"Look at me," he said, and then I did. His face was awash with sincerity. "The way you see the world," he said.

I tensed, my whole body ready for the accusation, for more of the same. But he surprised me.

"You're so easy to love," he said. "It would be so easy for you to find someone else who loved you."

His face, without its usual salesman's varnish, was disconcerting. He was scaring me. "Stop it," I said. He was reminding me of being alone, answering a question that had not been asked, and now the question, not the easily spoken answer, was what seemed true. The world without him whirled before my eyes, like some terrible rushing tide. There was something wrong with me, something wrong. "Please stop talking," I said, and held onto him for dear life.

And even now, a dissonance holds me upright, a faint but draining sense that something, like a tire or fan belt, may not hold. I grasp at things I learned in college, Jung saying when we couldn't stand to keep going forward we would go backward instead, looking for someone besides ourselves to blame. I remind myself wisely, over and over, that *Charlie* is the responsible one here—Charlie's anger, Charlie's strength, Charlie's two hands. It is physically impossible to spit in one's own face, I tell myself cleverly. And: It is part of the syndrome for the woman to feel it is her fault. That there is even a syndrome, that this happens everywhere, without reason, should comfort me, but it doesn't. The interstate stretches placidly ahead, shaded by a sweep of high clouds. The question sits, motionless, in the back of my mind: why I let this happen, what weakness in me caused this. Or is it something my mother should have seen in me, but forgot to see?

• • •

She never had counseling or went to any support groups when my father died, though her friends and relatives all urged her to. "Vocation and avocation," she said. "That's all the therapy I need." Once, in a stack of papers on her nightstand, I found a newspaper clipping about a group for new widows and widowers. The article featured a man who shaved his legs and held them in bed at night, "just to feel some soft skin," and a woman who wouldn't throw away her deceased husband's Jockey shorts. Anything you needed to do was okay, the article said. I was eleven or twelve when I found this, and it became a source of high, secret hilarity for my friends and me. We weren't laughing at these people's tragedies, it was just the Jockey shorts, though if my mother had seemed tragic, the article might have struck me differently. But she had begun selling her figurines in shopping centers and plazas, and sometimes taught pottery to small groups of women on our porch. And she laughed with me about the women after they left, saying one looked like she was carved out of a butcher's block, another should know better than to wear halter tops—these poor women who had nothing better to do than to take her class, these were the ones to feel sorry for.

It did seem odd that she didn't date, but by the time I noticed, I was dating, and much too involved to give my mother's lack of love life a second thought. And by that time, too, she was busy looking after the greasers. The boys I went out with, of course, weren't nearly as dramatic as the greasers; even then I chose regular boys who wore sweaters and had confidence in their futures, nothing for my mother to worry about. Senior year I went out with a Latvian boy I knew from Art Council who wore five earrings and always had some kind of foreign cigarette going when he came to our front door, but my mother liked him so much she gave him one of her homemade ashtrays for Christmas, a turtle with a sly, flirtatious tilt to its head. "There are worse things than smoking," she said, and did not elaborate. And the Latvian boy was, after all, harmless.

"Why don't you get a boyfriend?" I asked her finally, my first time home from college on a break.

"I hate old men," she said, smiling. "You know that."

I wonder now if she knew something I didn't when she made that remark, if she was trying to tell me something important about us or just making a joke.

• • •

It's well after dark when I stop in Seymour for coffee and mouthwash. Charlie always insists on Listerine, says it's "superior" even though gargling with it is actually painful, and I wish he could see me buying this tasty, sugary green brand. I want him to see me being kind to myself, and suffer. What I wish for, simply enough, is not his repentance, but his suffering. Memory and grudge are twin swamps to watch out for, I think. Even animals may be susceptible—my goldfish may be swimming in hate right now, wanting to kill me for leaving him alone with nothing but Charlie and a scallop-shaped vacation feeder. But somehow I doubt it, and I can now see why the fish and I always got along so well, the way he went along so easily, pumping waves of unconsciousness through his gills, never knowing or owning up to a thing.

Once, with Charlie, I came close to living in that state forever. While it was happening I was thinking about my Walk-
man and how it stopped tracking the tape after I dropped it
on concrete. I was picturing tiny wires coming apart, shaking
loose, picturing this while Charlie held my chin and cracked
the back of my head against the floor, over and over. And
suddenly all I knew was that I didn't *want* to be unconscious,
sunken into myself, my brain a fallen soufflé. At that moment
I promised someone, God or Jung or whoever was out there,
that I would work harder and be kinder and stop wearing mas-
cara and take more responsibility, whatever it took. It was my
fault that this was happening, my fault for loving my lazy, easy
life. "You asked for it," Charlie was probably saying—it was
what he always said—and I believed him.

I doze in my car for an hour in the lot of a Hardee's. I
dream that I am facing Charlie, just a few feet away from
him, and I'm holding a gun. I'm fully dressed and sobbing,
but the three women behind Charlie are nude and noncha-
lant. Charlie laughs, knowing I am afraid to shoot, that I don't
even know how. He starts walking toward me, slowly, slowly,
smiling, enjoying this. *I have no choice*, I cry at the last possible moment, and fire, falling as he falls, to the ground. Just
like that, he's dead. I am crying so hard I can barely see, barely
catch my breath. The nude women look on, disinterestedly. *It
wouldn't have bothered me to do that*, one of them says.

Rain wakes me—not the noise, but the quality of it. In the
South the summer rains are violent, but routinely so; they
come down daily in friendly torrents. Up here the storms are
more random. The raindrops are smaller and meaner, and they
pelt you according to some unseen plan. My windshield looks
like it's breathing. It reminds me of *The Last Wave*, where that
poor guy discovers he's the harbinger of the apocalyptic tidal
wave. Of course, he figures it out too late and it's all inevitable anyway, his image having been carved in stone by aborigi-
nes before he was even born. The first sign he gets is the rain,

though, and soon the water is everywhere, surrounding his car and seeping into his home, and when he finally understands, it is both too early and too late for him to do anything.

I am at a Hardee's, I remind myself, a Hardee's in southern Indiana, thinking about the riddle of fate. I turn on my wipers and merge back onto the highway, judging that it will be near dawn by the time I reach my mother's house. The easy authority of the talk-radio host reassures me. "I'm here to tell you: zoning is liquid," he tells a worried caller, and the caller begins to sound a little less worried.

• • •

It isn't light yet after all, when I get there, but it's not quite dark either. When I drive around the cul-de-sac the neighbors' security bulb flashes on, as it has for years. Somebody must be landscaping the copse in the center of the cul-de-sac, I notice, because it doesn't look any thicker. My mother's miniature pickup truck is parked in the center of the driveway. As I pull up I realize my big old Chevy will fit neither behind it nor beside it. "No problem," I say aloud. I know the hiding place for her truck keys. I stop where I am, in the street, and turn off the ignition. It still feels like something is running underneath me when I get out. The pavement feels like it might have a motor in it, vibrating slightly against the soles of my shoes. An early morning redwing sounds a single hoarse note. I slide my mother's truck keys out from beneath a clay pot of marigolds that sits beside the front steps.

The problem, once I'm in her truck, is that it's a stick shift, something I've never learned to do, and I can barely keep my eyes from blurring into sleep. I fumble with the clutch uncertainly, then fit my hand around the heavy grip and move it in a direction that feels right. The truck coughs and dies and rolls backward and I jerk my left leg up in surprise, banging my bruise against the dash. I brake hard and too late, and the truck's back end slams the side of my car with a final, metallic jolt. And that, apparently, is as much as I can take—my tears come boiling up, and I wrap my arms around the steering wheel and press myself into it, sobbing, sobbing. And then my mother is there, barefoot in her old Lanz nightgown, smelling of bacon, clay, and lotion soap, reaching in for me. "Oh, honey," she is saying. A long time goes by before I'm ready to go inside, but when I do finally look up the sky has begun to lighten, the house has begun to take on tentative colors.

At the last minute there is something that makes her hesitate. We'll look at the dent later, she says; first things first. But as we're walking up the driveway she looks quickly back over her shoulder at the truck. "What is it?" I say.

"Nope," she says, shaking her head. "Nothing."

"Mom," I say. "What?"

She looks at me closely for a moment and moves a lock of my hair. "Nothing," she says finally. "I just left a couple of new bud vases in the back. But it doesn't matter, honey—they weren't anything special."

"Mom," I say. "Come on. Let's go see how bad it is." I head back to the truck and she hurries up behind me.

"Honey," she says, "it really doesn't matter. I can always do those little bud vases. I'll clean it up later."

I put my foot on the bumper and hoist myself up into the back of the truck. The vases are wrapped in a canvas tarpaulin, and the bundle has slid to one end of the truck bed—it's smashed up next to a box of gardening tools. I open the canvas gingerly, expecting a mess, but the bud vases, for whatever they're worth, are still in one piece. I look up, relieved, but she has already turned her back. I can see the blond hairs on her arms lit up by the sun as she moves evenly toward the house, and I marvel at how young she looks still, as though nothing bad has ever happened to her.

the reverse phone book

Dallas's dream was to someday live in an apartment large enough for him and his dearest friends to whip through it on roller skates, screaming, "It's happening! It's happening!" at the moment of his triumph, but he was already thirty, lived alone on a waiter's salary, and had neither triumphs nor dear friends. His last friend had been his nearly silent college roommate, Chune Pei Liu, but Chune had gone to jail one night for uprooting and dragging a small holly tree across campus and then threatening the officers who tried to arrest him with kitchen knives, and he moved out without warning soon after that. He did not contact Dallas again, even though he left behind half his clothes and twenty Ramen Dinners and his Daisy Seal-A-Meal and a hairbrush full of hair. He must have undergone some sort of spiritual revelation or transformation, Dallas figured. He was mildly envious.

Dallas knew he should have a plan, but he didn't have one. He loved music but had never laid his hands on a single musical instrument of any kind. Still, he often stayed up late at night listening to his old clock-radio, watching the flapping digits until they blurred and picturing his own hidden talent someday shooting out of him like staples from a gun. "This could use an arpeggio," he liked to say, with authority, when listening. He loved arpeggios. He loved arpeggios and he adored the phrase WIDE LOAD. "WIDE LOAD, coming through!" he shouted whenever he had to carry a tray with more than three items on it out of the kitchen at the restaurant at which he worked. The restaurant was quite busy and so this happened several times each night, causing Dallas's coworkers to treat him as though he were a moron. He knew they thought he was a moron and yet he couldn't help himself.

Why was he given to such extravagance and exclamation? he wondered. Had he seen something, such as the Space Shuttle, explode when he was a child, and he just didn't remember it? He had read somewhere that the children who witnessed that event were given to conditions like his, a chronic unease with the normal pace and pitch of the world, something like motion sickness. They did things like bite the button eyes off their stuffed rabbits and choke, or grow up and refuse to move out of their parents' houses. But Dallas was sure he hadn't seen anything explode. Well, one time he had seen a potato his mother had failed to puncture explode in the oven but he loved that. "Poomp!" he had shouted at his mother, for weeks afterward.

He didn't know why he was the way he was, but he was beginning to feel like he'd spilled something on his own life, ruining it even before it was fully his. The feeling was familiar; as a child he had accidentally broken almost everything he touched, including most of his own belongings. His mother had referred to him in conversation as Destructo. When he was nine, his new pet guinea pig unexpectedly gave birth one night, all the babies stillborn but one, a brown-haired sleek little thing that hopped around the aquarium just hours after its birth, seemingly unconfused about what was required of it—but Dallas accidentally killed it the next day by dropping it behind a chest of drawers. It did not die right away but lay in the corner of the cage with its eyes open, sighing, for hours, Dallas watching it desperately through the glass. "I told you not to pick it up," his mother said, standing behind him. But it was so cute, how could he help himself? Destiny, he had named it, before he dropped it, because the mother had been carrying it around for so long without anyone knowing. And as it flipped out of his hands, behind the dresser, he felt the moment had already come, that it had been written down somewhere to wait for him.

As an adult Dallas still believed in fate, tried to recognize its clues and messages in his life, but he was beginning to see that fate was not, had never been, his friend. The simplest of pleasant events escaped him. He could not even get a girl to go out with him.

Suzanne, the girl he wanted, worked as a server with him at the restaurant, though she also had another duty there which made her seem to Dallas hopelessly, unreachably superior: she described the daily specials to people who called in to place their orders on the telephone. The restaurant, though located near an industrial park in the ugly, empty part of town, offered progressive entrees made up of ingredients one would never expect to find together on the same continent, let alone in the same baking pan, and so Suzanne, using her precise, highly credible voice, would explicate the recipes to the wary. Whenever she was called upon to do this, Dallas managed to stop what he was doing and listen. If he was delivering a tray full of steaming plates he would pause by the front desk where the phone was and pretend to rearrange a fruit garnish. "What would you like described?" Suzanne always said. The sexual innuendoes suggested by this kind of talk were so obvious that no one, not even the giddy waitresses who were Suzanne's buddies, bothered to make them, but Dallas always felt when he heard her that an evil cartoon sex fiend ghost, something like the Tasmanian Devil, was inside of him, trying to punch its way out.

Suzanne, like everyone else, thought Dallas was a fool. When he spoke to her her pretty lips flattened into an impatient line, and twice he'd seen her roll her eyes at the mention of his name. Her boyfriend, a long-haired classical cellist, picked her up each night at closing time, the heroic weight of his instrument hanging all around him like a cloud of scent. He looked like Robin Hood, bounding sensitively in and out of the restaurant. Dallas knew there was no way he could compete.

Once, before Robin Hood had started showing up, Dallas had had Suzanne over to his apartment for pork medallions. He had taken advantage of the fact that she had only been working with him a week, knowing she was bound to fall in with the rest of the staff sooner or later. The knowledge that he'd had to resort to this strategy sat like an undissolved lozenge at the back of his throat the day of their date, and he passed by the shabby Winn-Dixie where he usually shopped and drove four miles across town to Publix, where an amazing thing happened: while he was standing in the checkout line, a bird sailed by overhead, disappearing into the wall of houseplants that fronted the produce section. Dallas looked around, and a few other people looked around with him, blinking in a blank sort of way. A moment later the bird sailed back over their heads, a regular brown bird like you would see outside, and a woman in front of Dallas said, "Whose job is it to take care of that?" Before anyone could answer, the bird sailed over a third time, crashed into the glass wall near the exits, and fell open-winged to the floor. Without thinking about it, Dallas sprinted over to the stunned bird and threw his windbreaker on it and took it outside, where he deposited it under a hedge that bordered the lot. Then he jogged back in and paid for his groceries and went home.

By the time Suzanne arrived, he could barely contain himself, he had been thinking about the incident all afternoon. He took Suzanne's jacket, told her about the bird, and imitated for her the response of the checkout girl: "'When I saw you running for the bird, I said, *There's a man of action!*'" Suzanne seemed to smile. He was sure she had smiled. As he brought out their beers and Li'l Smokies he said, "You know, the truly amazing thing was how nobody wanted to be the one to say they saw it. Just like when someone gets murdered in New York City in front of everyone but nobody says, *Hey, you know, cut that out*. Not that I've ever been there, but you know what I mean?" Suzanne looked pretty, biting daintily at her wienie, he thought. "Of course, you never realize how big these stores really are until you see a bird in there," he told her, over their main course. "I mean, it was really *flying*. It had a long way to *go*." Then, during dessert, he worried again about whether the bird would be permanently traumatized, whether other birds would smell person on it, etc. "The bush I left it under was pretty small," he said. "It did *hop*, but I'm thinking maybe I should have taken it across the street to the park . . ."

Suzanne suddenly said, "If I hear the word 'bird' one more time, I'm walking out that door." Dallas was surprised and a little embarrassed.

"Okay," he said. Only then, a moment later, he remembered the most miraculous thing, which he hadn't yet told her. "I'm sorry," he said quickly and conspiratorially, "but I forgot to tell you the most amazing part: I could feel the *you-know-what's* heart beating! Through my windbreaker, I could feel it in my hand! It was so fast you couldn't even make out separate beats!"

Suzanne flung down her napkin and left.

He thought immediately of calling her, then thought of how much better a note would be and, leaving their plates of red velvet cake on the table, ran to the closet and lugged out the Smith-Corona he'd received for his high school graduation and set it up on the floor beside an outlet. He would explain, the elite typeface lending dignity to his words, that she had not seen the real him. He wasn't himself, it was that simple. It was like that post-traumatic stress thing, the Space Shuttle thing, reactivated by seeing the bird (though the bird didn't explode). He would not pass her the note childishly at work but send it through the mail, bespeaking civility, self-control, *breeding*. He began to type, but a second later stopped: he didn't know her address, not even her last name! Her phone number was all he had.

Then, in a flash, he remembered the reverse phone book—Chune Pei Liu had told him about it once in the middle of the night—a phone book that would tell you, if you had a number, who the person was that it belonged to, and of course where they lived. The book was top secret, Chune said; only phone company officials were allowed to see it, but he had managed to get a copy, and now it was gone. He would be sent to jail! he'd yelled at Dallas. He was searching the place frantically, pulling up the edges of the carpet and dragging the refrigerator away from the wall; he pushed Dallas out of bed so he could check between the mattress and the box spring. In the morning, though, he was a little confused. Maybe he'd only dreamed that he had a copy, he said. Or maybe he'd dreamed that the book existed in the first place.

Dallas sighed. The local white pages were short, only one or two hundred pages—how long could it possibly take to skim through, if he looked only at first names and 335 prefixes? He sat Indian-style for an hour or so, running his finger down the columns, sometimes going back and rereading a page when he thought his mind might have wandered, but he didn't find anyone who could have been her. Finally he gave up and went to bed.

Dallas still thought about the evening all the time, though it had been over a year ago. He saw Suzanne almost every day, and sometimes she smiled and sometimes she didn't. He kept waiting for the right thing to say to her to leap into his mind, but the thing remained obscure, even cagey. He sometimes began to feel that the thing should not have to be an apology, that none of this was his fault, that there was no logical reason why he should not be allowed some gratification in the world, but the thing itself seemed to rebel at this show of independence on Dallas's part, assuring him that whatever he came up with would be wrong, and that anyone, everyone, most particularly Suzanne, would know it.

• • •

ATTENTION: BUG PEOPLE, said the mailing label he'd lettered and stuck on his front door, warning the exterminator that he was allergic to every kind of spray, but when he got home from work one Friday night he heard noises in there anyway and realized with disappointment that Donna Long was there. He just wanted to be alone—he'd relayed three phone messages from Robin Hood to Suzanne that evening, which he had hoped meant they were breaking up but which had turned out to mean that they were planning a camping trip. "I could take care of your cats while you're away," Dallas had said to her, but she'd only laughed.

Donna's car, a swanky royal-blue 1966 Chevy Impala, must have been parked in the back. The car was always larger than Dallas believed possible, and it embarrassed him a little, as though Donna were not the building's plumber but some backwards friend of his who had come to stay. She had been trying to fix his slow shower drain off and on for eight weeks, and he felt that this reflected on him personally, on some embarrassing defect of his body or character. She sometimes went out for a chemical or part and returned eight hours later as "The Tonight Show" was coming on, or eight days later, out of nowhere. He coughed as he let himself in; he felt he had to appear soberly busy with important tasks at all times whenever a maintenance or repair person was in his home.

"Yoo-hoo!" Donna Long yelled from the bathroom. "I finally got my hands on that clog, and you won't believe what it was."

Dallas stood in the doorway and watched Donna's broad bent back straining the seams of her plaid flannel shirt. From the back, she could have been a man. She had one arm deep in a fresh hole she had made in the tiled wall. "Six-inch stopper chain," she said, into the hole. "Wound around enough hair to build King Kong.

Hair would've gone, but no chemical I know eats through a *chain*."

"So that's it, you're done?" Dallas said.

"Not quite, dude," she said. "Got some reassembling to do." She withdrew her arm slowly and he looked away, as though he might have seen something obscene. When he looked back she had straightened up to her full height of six feet and stood there grinning at him and holding her black hand away from her body. She looked like an oversized baby doll, he thought, and he noticed that her face appeared worse than usual, her eyes unusually bright and damaged-looking.

"I see you looking at that," she said, touching the skin under one of her eyes, "but you don't need to get alarmed. I just had a little conflict with my sister the other night. Debbie. She's a big bruiser like myself. She been staying with me at my trailer since her old man run off, and she gets to drinking, you know what I mean?"

Dallas nodded and quickly retreated into the kitchen, embarrassed. "Yup, Debbie don't like Debbie, *that's* the problem," he could hear her saying. "Debbie got to learn to like Debbie *first*." The way she kept talking to herself reminded him of the endless family of gray cats who lived near the dumpster behind the restaurant and spent their days and nights strolling around and crying, begging, never getting enough of whatever it was they wanted. They were cute cats, but nobody ever took one in. Their wiggly bodies and bright eyes, which would have seemed adorable on other, calmer cats, seemed, oddly, only to make them more pathetic, even slightly grotesque.

Donna clanked around in her toolbox for a moment and then began to hum in a high, surprisingly feminine voice. Dallas got a Baggie full of yogurt-dipped peanuts from the refrigerator and stood in his kitchen, eating them one at a time and listening. The tune arrested him. It was slow and sad in an old-fashioned, respectable way, as though whoever wrote it took sadness for granted. He didn't think he'd heard it before, but it reminded him of a golden summer twenty years ago when he had become obsessed with stamp collecting. He remembered crouching over his album on the sunny floor of his bedroom for days on end until the muscles in the backs of his knees got sore and he could hardly stand without falling down. And then came a terrible evening when he had almost fainted in his bed when he felt a stray stamp hinge tickling his ankle and believed for a moment that it was a black widow. "I told you not to overdo it," his mother had said. Donna's sad, wordless vibrato was bringing this all back to him.

"What song is that?" he called to her.

"What'd you say, honey?" Donna yelled.

Dallas headed down the dark hall, shouting, "What *song* is that?" and slammed into Donna's flannel front. He leaped backwards.

"'I Missed Me,'" she said.

"You missed me?" Dallas said.

"No, the song is 'I Missed Me,'" she said. "The legendary late Jim Reeves. I ordered it off the TV."

"Oh," Dallas said. "I listen to classical music."

"Well, I don't know if you'd call it a *classic*, but it sure sticks with you," Donna said. "Had it in my head for a week. Even dreamed it."

"Uh huh," Dallas said. He was embarrassed to be standing so close to her in the dark.

"Hey, what are you eating there?" she said.

He offered her a yogurt peanut.

She chewed with concentration and her eyes widened. "Dude!" she said. "These are *great!*" She stared at him disbelievingly, as though he personally had been hiding all yogurt peanuts from her her whole life.

"You can have them, take them," he said.

"*Thank* you!" she said.

"So you're coming back to seal that up?" he said.

"Yeah, tomorrow," she said. "But where do you *get* these?"

"Any grocery store," Dallas said, edging back toward the front door.

"Well, good night," she finally said. "Dude, yogurt! I just can't get over that!"

Dallas got into his pajamas, trying without success to whistle the song. He realized a moment later that he had forgotten to ask her whether he was allowed to shower.

• • •

"Your Uncle Lafitte was always a melancholy man," his mother told him on the phone the next morning. "Laughing on the outside, crying on the inside, as they say. But when he went on the road, he became a new man." She was implying that Dallas took after Lafitte, but Lafitte had died of tequila poisoning when Dallas was still very little, and Dallas barely remembered the man. He had seen him maybe once, at someone's wedding. He had a picture in his head of a stout, gleaming man in a crisp white shirt and trousers that looked like they'd been assembled out of bedsheets, sitting heavily in a straight-backed chair next to a buffet table on which was an enormous silver urn full of whipped cream. Dallas made several trips to the table to gaze up at the whipped cream, whose merry peaks he could just see rising above the rim of the urn, and every time he approached the table his Uncle Lafitte was making a pronouncement. "Well, you might be in the water, but you sure ain't getting *wet*, you know what I mean?" Uncle Lafitte roared. "Well, you might be breathing, but you sure ain't getting any *air*, you know what I mean?" he shouted. "Well, you might be on the highway, but that ain't your *car*, you know what I'm saying?" Dallas had no picture in his head of the person to whom his uncle was speaking. He had, in fact, a suspicion that the whole memory was false, that like the reverse phone book it was only a dream.

"Take a lesson from Lafitte," Dallas's mother said. "On the road, he found what he was looking for all those years." Before his death, Uncle Lafitte had invented, marketed, and made famous throughout the Panhandle a powder that took the itch right out of your skin. He had sold a riding mower to a blind man who had bumped into it while trying to find the store's rest room. He'd sold a stereo system to an old couple so deaf they had to lie on the floor of the store with their heads next to the speakers in order to hear anything. But Dallas knew no one would ever buy anything from him, and he felt anyway that his own life must be stupid peas compared to whatever would make a man drink tequila. He hated tequila. If Lafitte were alive, he would probably pace once around Dallas's tiny apartment and spit. "What is your exact problem this instant?" Dallas's mother said.

"I can't take a shower," Dallas said.

After he hung up with his mother he immediately dialed Donna Long. "When am I allowed to take a shower?" he said, as soon as she answered.

"This ain't Donna," the woman's voice said.

"Great," Dallas said. "Well, I have to go to work, so where is she?"

"You that Texas guy?" the woman said. "Boy, I'm still waiting to hear the end of *you*. You better watch it. Wink at her once and she'll be moving in the piano, the chandelier, and all the fine china."

"Wait, oh my God," Dallas said. "Donna has a piano?"

"Figure of speech," the woman said. "I'll give her your message." She hung up.

Dallas went to his shower and looked at the hole. It was the size of two tiles and its edges were uneven with crumbling drywall and bits of mildewed caulking. It reminded him of a wound. He couldn't even imagine what it would be like to put his hand into it.

He worked the lunch shift unshowered, his forehead shining with oil. He could certainly have washed his face in his sink, but this hadn't occurred to him at the time. Feeling oily, he was subdued and preoccupied, and a couple of Suzanne's buddies started calling him "Mr. Business." Suzanne herself kept her usual distance, though this time Dallas felt that Donna, rather than he himself, was to blame.

He had a full three hours off between lunch and dinner, but he drove back to his apartment weaving and swearing as though someone were having his baby there. The Impala shone snazzily under a maple. "Thank *God,*" Dallas said.

Inside, he heard low quick talking, a hoarse unfamiliar voice. But he could see Donna's heavy legs, it had to be her. She was sitting on his bed, using his phone. "No, because I'll be gone," she was saying. "I'm fixing to leave, do you understand me? *Goodbye,* dude." But she didn't hang up. Her voice sounded like a little girl's. "I would *too,*" she said. "Texas. So think about that. You didn't think about that, did you? Did you? I didn't think you did."

Dallas stood in the bedroom doorway and pretended to sneeze.

"Dude, shit," Donna said, and hung up so hard that the ringer dinged. Her face was wet, guilty, desperate. She stared past him, over him, then back at the floor.

"It's okay, you can use the phone, it wasn't long distance, was it?" Dallas said. Her face looked swollen, distorted in places, and he forgot what he'd been planning to say.

"It was local," she sobbed. She bent her head down over her knees and her yellow doll hair made a smooth upside-down bowl. "I'm sorry, I'm sorry," she cried into her knees.

"Hey, whatever," Dallas said. He was relieved that her blackened eyes were now hidden from his view. Nothing about her crying here in his bedroom seemed real. He had no idea what was required of him.

"Nothing ever works out for me," she cried into her knees. "It's not fair, man, you know?"

"Maybe if you didn't try so hard," Dallas said. "You know, you're a pretty intense person."

She snapped her head up and looked at him. "What the hell are you talking about?" she said.

"I just mean, you know, you might be giving people the wrong impression," he said. "People get uncomfortable . . ."

She rose and pushed past him in a wind of deodorant soap. "I'll come back," she muttered.

He stood for a while in the middle of his living room when she was gone. Finally he went and checked the bathroom, but the hole was still there, gaping at him. He stared at it, squinting, trying to see it as smaller, but it wasn't. It was an innocent-looking hole, but he could picture the geyser that might explode from it, should he turn on the faucet. Then a terrible thought came to him and he sat down on the edge of the bathtub.

It could not be her sister punching her. He'd *seen* her sister once, and she was tiny, she looked twelve. How could he have forgotten? She had come by to drop off some pliers Donna had forgotten, and when he saw her coming up the walk he had thought she was a Girl Scout coming with cookies. It was a *man* hurting her, someone like Bill Laimbeer, the kind of man Lafitte would have whipped, would have laughed at Dallas for not whipping—he pictured her trailer littered with broken dishes, like in a TV movie. Poor Donna! He looked back at the hole. *Unless Donna has another sister,* the hole seemed to say.

He went quickly to his telephone, glancing over his shoulder as though he were going to steal something. He dialed Donna's number, craning his neck to keep an eye on the front door, in case she should come back in with her passkey. He didn't think to plan what to say, and when the woman's twangy voice suddenly said, "Hello," he was startled.

"How big are you?" he whispered.

"Jesus Christ," she said, and hung up.

This sobered him. There was nothing to do but go back to work. He thought of leaving her a note: *I didn't mean anything bad by what I said. Take your time with the shower. I will do whatever I can to help.* And maybe he would do something small in the meantime, like get her some more peanuts. He ran a damp washcloth over his face and up and down his arms, whistling a quick, nervous version of what he was sure was "I Missed Me." The end part sounded like "Pop Goes the Weasel," but the rest he was sure he had down. He smelled good, and except for his hair, which waved unnaturally out on the sides like wings, he looked fine. He was dying to tell someone about the drama all around him and he drove back to work as wildly as he'd driven home.

"You look different," Suzanne remarked to him during a lull.

He could not remember her ever initiating a conversation before, but tonight it didn't surprise him. "I know," he said. "You wouldn't believe what's been going on with my shower."

"I thought you got your hair cut," Suzanne said, yawning. She was leaning against an empty wine rack in the kitchen, looking as though she wanted to go take a nap.

"No, but I've been helping my friend Donna," Dallas said. "Her husband's a Neanderthal. I think he's some kind of trucker. She's been staying with me. She said she feels safer that way." He had not known he was going to say any of this until he said it, but as he said it it seemed true.

"That's nice," Suzanne said, and yawned.

"It was the least I could do," Dallas said.

"Uh huh," Suzanne said. She shut her eyes, showing pearl-shaded lids.

"Hey, can I ask you something?" Dallas said. He wanted her to open her eyes.

"What?" she said. Her lids did not twitch.

"Do I smell different to you?" he said. He thrust his wrist under her nose, actually brushing it against her soft upper lip. He was aware that it was the first time he'd ever touched her.

She jerked back, knocking the wooden rack over against the wall. "Get away from me!" she said. Two white-aproned cooks turned their heads and stared.

Dallas lowered his arm and stood there. Suzanne blushed and busily righted the wine rack, not looking at him. "Phone!" someone called from the front, and she shot through the silver swinging door. Dallas waited for the door to stop swinging, ignoring the cooks, who were still watching him, and went and stared at Suzanne through the door's greasy porthole. He could see her profile, her lips moving in a measured way, but he couldn't hear her over the noise of the mixers and kitchen fans. He felt a blush deep in him that wanted to rise to his face, but something heavy and stubborn was holding it down.

• • •

He had forgotten to leave any lights on. He walked through the dark to his room and went directly to bed. The heaviness in him was like a fever, and he fell into a busy, dreaming sleep. He was with Robin Hood, riding on an old upright piano that was sinking into a swamp. They were trying to get to Suzanne, but they got everywhere too late. They boarded a plane the shape of a needle, but the plane would not fly with Dallas on it. Then he was at the wedding again, watching Lafitte and the knowing, unreachable whipped cream. "Don't just stand there," Lafitte shouted at him. "Grab her now before your grab is gone!" Lafitte's eyes bulged whitely, and Dallas jumped back, horrified. The man was dead. He turned and Donna was right behind him, her flannel arms open, and he pressed himself into them, sobbing. The flannel smelled like a memory. "Let me stay with you," he sobbed, his throat aching, and she tightened her arms around him, pressing him close to her large body.

He woke up sweating, deeply embarrassed. He thought immediately of quitting his job. He wondered if what he'd done to Suzanne could legally be considered anything. He was pretty sure it could not be, but this didn't make him feel any better. He had until dinner to decide what to do.

In the bathroom the smooth wall shocked him. It was perfect, not even a crumb of putty, as though nothing had ever happened. He touched the tile as gingerly as if it were a face, then turned on the faucet to make sure it worked. A pink Post-It note was stuck on the mirror: *Sorry for the inconvenience—forgot to say it was OK to use it. I meant to tell you. Have a nice day. Donna Long.*

"Thank you," he said aloud, running his hands under the hot water. The water felt wonderful, better than regular water, and he felt something turn over in his chest. He wanted to thank her. He had to thank her. He left the tap on and ran to the bedroom, the telephone. They would take a trip! They would drive off to Texas together in the royal-blue Chevy called Destiny. They would sit in the roomy front seat together like grandparents, enjoying enormous Texas sunsets through the windshield. They could even sleep in the car if they had to, in each other's arms, and having finally caught up with fate, he would be reminded of nothing at all when he smelled her soapy, flannel smell. They would leave Suzanne and Robin Hood and the restaurant and the trailer full of broken dishes behind them forever. He would do all the cooking.

"She's gone," the woman's flat voice said.

"You mean she went out?" Dallas said. "When will she be back?"

"She left town," the woman said. "But she said she got you all taken care of."

"No, this isn't about my drain," Dallas said. "Where did she go? Vacation?"

"She just left," the woman said. "I don't see that it's any of your business. You got another problem with your drain?"

"No!" Dallas shouted.

"I'll give her your message," the woman said, and hung up.

Dallas sat on the bed, his heart still pounding, the water still rushing in the bathroom. He was not going to give up. It was different this time, he knew her last name, he wouldn't need the reverse phone book, even if there were one. He could follow her, or he could wait. If he waited, surely she'd come back. And if she didn't come back right away, he could quit his job anyway. He didn't ever have to see Suzanne again. He didn't ever have to return. His heart pounded all around him, filling the apartment with sound and movement. He had until the dinner shift to decide what to do.

undisclosed location

I said yes to Borden's proposition because I was vulnerable; I'd just been turned down for a job at the local rodeo as one of the girls in shorts and boots who get the crowd excited by pretending to rescue the clowns from the bull. I was after some color and action, anything but typing, and I already owned a pair of quality boots, but this was an insider's job—you had to know a cowboy, or at least a clown. Plenty of girls had hand-tooled, snake-trimmed boots like mine, or so the smirking rodeo administrator said. He seemed not to like my looks. So, back home, when fat Borden hissed at me from his doorway, his big gleaming face and shirtfront filling the crack between door and jamb, I stopped. Usually I tried to cat-foot across his landing, a tough trick on our building's old hollow hardwood stairs, but this time I was already resigned, and still wearing my fancy, clunky boots from the rodeo interview.

"Hey, CeCe, stop a minute," he said. "Where you been? Those are nice boots you got, none of that endangered shit, right? Listen, I got something you ain't gonna believe." He always said this, and it could mean anything: macaroons, a ceiling leak, new mollies in his tank, Kristy McNichol all grown up on TV. He worked late nights watching over the parking lot of a small-time chemical plant, and spent his days, as far as I could tell, sauntering heavily around his apartment, turning his appliances off and on and looking out the window. When I came up the block he would often appear there, wave, and then let the curtain fall briskly, as though he had to get back to some top secret business or lingerie model in his bed. Of course I knew that wasn't the case—his girlfriend showed up sometimes in the afternoons, and she was faded-looking, bottom-heavy. She wore a droopy uniform tied with an orange sash, and her name, Frieda, in orange italics across the breast pocket, and though I recognized this as some fast-food getup, I hoped vaguely for his sake that she was something more like a crossing guard—kind, maternal, respectable.

"What can I do for you, Borden?" I said. The canned spaghetti smell of his apartment drifted out and surrounded us, filling the hall.

"Well, as a matter of fact, I noticed you been around a lot lately, and I thought maybe you were between jobs."

"Actually, this is my paid vacation," I told him. It was true. I'd set an office record by holding the position of typist for three years, so they'd given me this—nothing sparkly or engraved, but a week. Borden didn't have to know how I was spending it, looking for work in rodeos and water parks and petting zoos.

"Well, more power to you," he said. "God bless. You enjoy yourself, okay?" He ran a crumpled, cornucopia-patterned paper towel over his brow.

I could have gotten away then, but for some reason I asked him what he had wanted.

He flushed, lit up. "I need a house-sitter," he said. "Starting Monday, for a month. Maybe your cute friend with the Mantra? She sure is a sweet thing." He meant my best friend Jeannie, who was pointy and petite and drove an Opel Manta.

"She's full-time at the bank now, and she's busy planning her wedding," I said. "So she's not available. So what's up, Borden? Everything okay? Where are you going?" In two years I doubted he'd ever spent more than twelve hours at a stretch away from his place.

"Undisclosed location," he said. He glowed strangely; drugs occurred to me.

"What are you talking about?" I said. "Are you sick?"

"No, just trust me," he said. "Why do you always look so suspicious? Jeez, you're like what's her name, 'Murder She Wrote.' Listen, you just gotta keep up the aquarium. I'll give you seven bucks a week, that's a buck a day. You don't have to stay here or nothing. I know you got a busy life. You can bring your cute friend over if you want, though."

I pictured Jeannie's evil grin, her small hands rifling through his personal belongings. She referred to him as Elsie. "Okay, Borden," I said. "Show me what you want me to do."

"I gotta show you later," he said. "I got a meeting." He stepped out and shut and locked his door. I stood there on the landing watching his fat back, his baggy hips retreating down the stairs. *FBI,* I thought. *America's Most Wanted. Something Anonymous. Betty Ford.*

The next morning, there he was, unbelievably, in the paper, holding a giant reproduction of a check from Florida Lotto like a clown's prop: 2.4 million dollars. His happy, grainy face was the size of my thumb. *Thomas Borden,* read the caption, *thirty-two,* and I was shocked; I'd thought that Borden was his only name—like Dopey or Dumbo—and also that he was years and years older than me. There was no story, only the paragraph-long caption, which noted that this particular win was especially poignant and thrilling because of the death of Borden's parents in a house fire four years previous. Things were finally taking a turn for the better for Borden. He was quoted: "My advice to everyone is keep playing Lotto, don't give up. You never know when the ball will start to roll in your direction." His grin looked knowing and wholesome, instead of fat and sad.

"Seven bucks a week," I said out loud. I thought of my mother, who'd recently had to have a marble-sized lump removed, and then there was a distant cousin of mine whose baby got a fever and could now no longer speak: *I* deserved to win. But those items weren't bad enough to go in a caption, and neither were the real items of my life: my stuck-up sailor boyfriend getting sick of me, for instance, saying he had to "move on" because I "lacked serious ambition," when I'd only started dating him as a joke, a game, something to tell Jeannie—sailor seeming as believable a profession to me as pirate or lion tamer or Indian chief. Or the rodeo man, a stranger, deciding I was too ugly to save clowns. Or Jeannie, the wild one of us, shopping for rings with her professor. Looking at Borden's smudgy 2-D face, I felt panic, realizing that if he won, no one else I knew could ever win; Borden, only Borden, was the one among us who deserved to win.

I could hear his phone ringing as soon as I stepped into the hallway, and when I got down there it was impossible to talk to him. He opened the door for me but ran back to the kitchen, where he was trying to rig up an answering machine which the ringing phone kept fouling. The machine was a cheap model, I noticed, the same brand as my blow-dryer. For a moment I actually pitied Borden. "Big congratulations," I said.

"Yeah, thanks," he said. Drops of sweat fell from his brow onto the blinking, clicking machine. "You're not gonna have to worry about this, once I get it hooked up."

"That was a pretty smart idea," I told him. "Leaving town."

"You bet," he said. "The Lotto Commission advises it. To avoid unwanted solicitations and attention. From acquaintances, you know."

"Are you taking Frieda?" I asked. She was the only person I ever saw going in and out of his place, and I imagined she would look healthier with a nice tan to set off her hair. I wished that for her, honestly.

"Even that I can't say," Borden said. "But I sure wouldn't mind taking your friend. Listen, you mind if I just give you the key and show you the brine shrimp? I'm kind of busy. I think I'm gonna leave tonight. I really appreciate this, CeCe."

"Oh, no problem, I'm just so happy for you," I said.

"Okay," he said. "Now, you ever hear the expression 'Your eyes are bigger than your stomach'? 'Cause what you got to remember here is that the fishes' stomachs are *small,* you know what I'm saying? If you look at their eyeballs, you'll see what I'm saying." He held his hand up to my face and showed me his finger and thumb pressed together, as though he were holding a tiny, invisible bead. Together we looked significantly at the invisible bead. Seconds went by, and finally he shook his head. "Jeez," he said, "you just never know when the ball's gonna roll your way."

• • •

"Well, the fat's in the fire now!" Jeannie shouted when I told her. Her voice was spotty with static because she was on the cellular phone the professor had given her, on her way to lunch at some Pavilion place. She always called from her car, even though the phone on her desk at the bank was unmonitored and had a hundred special features and worked fine, and she always shouted the whole time and complained about the bad traffic she was stuck in. We'd known each other too long for her to be showing off, but that's what it was—like complaining that she looked too young and was always getting carded. She wanted me to say, again, how special the professor was, how lavish, but I refused. He was petite like her, always looked like he'd had his hair cut that same day, and spoke to me in a measured, modest little voice, as though my big bones offended him, as though my neurons and dendrites were large and ungainly and an embarrassment to neuroscience, his honorable chosen field. Delicate, well-groomed men often treated me this way, as though I were likely to breathe up all their air or just fall on them like a tree, but when Roger did it I had to pretend not to notice—we were supposed to become great barbecue buddies, in-laws practically. And yet even gleeful Jeannie toned herself down around him, I'd observed. He couldn't possibly appreciate the real Jeannie, the Jeannie I'd known all my life.

Now, on the car phone, she was her regular self, shouting that I should have drunk the Riunite. She meant the night I moved into my apartment, when Borden opened his door eight or nine times during my trips up and down the stairs, not offering to help but pretending to check different things: the mail, his dead bolt, a bulb that hung over the landing. After a half-hour of this he finally affected to notice me, and brought out the bottle. "You look like you deserve a glass of this," he said. I shook his damp hand and told him I was allergic to sulfites. "Oh, yeah," he said, "I saw that on 'Sixty Minutes.'"

"You'd be having millionaire babies now, boy!" Jeannie yelled.

"Okay, okay," I said, and invited her over later to hang out at his place, to sit in the apartment of a millionaire.

"I'll break my hip in his bathroom and sue!" she shouted.

"But don't invite anybody else this time, okay?" I said. "We don't want things to get out of hand. Reporters might be lurking around, or other, more dangerous people."

"Alone's better, actually," she yelled, "because I need to talk to you some more about my wedding." She hung up, and the rush of her traffic was cut off with a click. My living room swelled with quiet. I remembered I needed to launder my lace-collar dress to wear to work, where they planned to take my picture for the newsletter, for having earned this bonus. Only Saturday and

Sunday were left of my vacation. If I shut my eyes I could see the days, like empty boxes, lined up in front of me.

• • •

We had all of Borden's bug-flecked lights turned on, a bottle of his bargain gin opened in the kitchen, and we'd switched off the ringer on the phone; the little answering machine was clicking away on a corner table like the Little Engine That Could, silently recording messages. A pizza was supposedly on the way, though we'd had to fight with the man on the phone, who said he'd taken half a dozen orders for this address already. "A hundred pizzas," he said. "A pizza with dollar bills on it. A Beluga pizza. Jesus, you think I'm an idiot?"

"Look, we only want *one*," I finally said. "We're using a *coupon*." That had worked.

Jeannie was twirling shoeless across the rug, her lacy slip flashing white, and I remembered meeting her for the first time in fourth grade, her wearing slips under her plain school dresses even then, as though she were better than the rest of us. "I'm spiking these guppies," she said, waving her drink over the tank.

"Check out their eyeballs first," I said. I was slumped on Borden's low yellow sofa, my cheek pressed against the worn velour, which smelled, up close, not like spaghetti but like a stuffed terrycloth pony I'd carried around everywhere until I was eight or nine years old. I had sucked on its matted yarn tail whenever I needed it, and when foam pieces started leaking from the rump, my mother cut the tail off for me to keep and threw the body in the trash. I took gulps of Borden's cheap gin, recalling how I had imagined the pony's body being absorbed by the roots of a nice tree somewhere, being soaked up and incorporated into the trunk of the tree, the nicest thing I could imagine happening to trash.

"Liven up, will you?" Jeannie said.

"I'm just wondering what stupid Borden is going to do with all that money," I said.

"Well, let's listen to that answering machine. Can't we just turn up the volume, without messing things up?"

"You better do it," I said. "You know how to use a car phone. You know how to use a safe-deposit box. I can't even get a job at the rodeo."

Jeannie gave me a look and adjusted the machine, which was in the middle of taping a message. "Mack Fine," a man's voice said. "Fine, Breen, and Janky, financial consultants. Flexibility is really what we're all about, so don't feel limited, say, by the list of services you see in our flyer." The doorbell buzzed.

"It's Janky!" Jeannie screamed.

I let in the flat-haired delivery girl, who was holding the pizza box propped against her hip like an empty cocktail tray. "Large mushroom onion," she said. "Ain't you the lottery girls?"

"We is," Jeannie said, "but you ain't gettin' no big tip."

"We flipped coins over who got to deliver this one," the pizza girl said. "They at least want the lowdown on you two. You know the guy who won, right?"

"I do," I said.

"I does," Jeannie said.

The pizza girl shook her head, and her stringy hair swung slowly. "What I wouldn't give," she said. "What's he like? Is he your old man?"

"Oh, well," I said, feeling my gin a little, in the way I kept nodding my head to the rhythm of her swinging hair. "He's a big guy, a stay-at-home kind of guy . . ."

". . . Dr. Stopes, I don't know if you remember me," came a sudden nasal voice from the answering machine. The three of us stood still and listened. "The Dermatology Lab in St. Paul. You were here last March? How are your nevi doing, have you had any recurrences? Anyway, all of us here just wanted to say, you know, congratulations." A high female voice yelped in the background. "Patty, who takes your appointments? Says congratulations. Anyway, we have some new samples of that fluoroplex generic we can send your way, so if you're interested you can give us a call at your convenience. Congratulations again." The machine clicked off and reset itself.

"Man, doctor wants to do you a *favor*," said the pizza girl.

"Why are you even still standing here?" Jeannie said to her.

"That was compassionate," I said to Jeannie after we'd let the girl out. I was back on the smelly couch, picking the oily onions, her idea, off my slice.

"Me?" she said. "What's wrong with you anyway? You're probably turning into *Mrs. Borden* sitting on that couch."

"And I'm also sick of looking at that Victoria's Secret shit, by the way," I said. "Am I supposed to be *aroused* or something?"

She came over and stood in front of me and raised her skirt, holding the hem by two fingers so that her slip hung there in my face. I felt like I was watching a blank projection screen, waiting for a movie to start. I remembered a fight we'd had in fourth or fifth grade in which I had called her "prostitute" and she had refused to reply, to that or to any of my insults, except to say, "Good." That had been our last real fight, now that I thought of it. "Is this how you're going to behave at your big important *wedding?*" I said.

"You're not really joking, are you?" she said. She looked at me and let her skirt fall. "Well," she said, after a while, "and I don't even feel bad telling you this, anymore, the way you're acting, but you're no longer maid of honor. Roger's sister is back in the country." Roger's sister didn't like Jeannie and had once given her a bad haircut on purpose.

"You could have just told me that on your *cellular*," I said. "In fact, you could tell your whole life story on your *cellular*." In a flash I saw Jeannie and me on the school playground in our green Girl Scout uniforms, forming the letters of the alphabet with our small, slender bodies, acting out for own amusement the physical progression from *A* to *B* to *C*, cocking our knees and elbows at bizarre angles, getting tangled in our sashes and laughing so hard at each other that we couldn't speak. For the first time, I saw that I had always operated on the unconscious assumption that our slow, steady movement away from childhood was arbitrary—that, like an amusement park ride, time would eventually pause, or halt, or even reverse itself and take us back in the other direction.

I heard the fierce scrape of Jeannie striking a match in the kitchen. "You can't smoke in here!" I yelled. "Borden says the mollies—*not guppies*—won't breed properly!" I had to take practically a whole breath to say each word, as though something large, an invisible Borden, had settled down on me; it was hard to hold things in my mind. A woman's voice on the answering machine was saying something about never forgiving, and I thought: security. Then I realized I had them reversed; the phone woman was talking about securities. "Never forgiving" had come from me. A knock that seemed to have been going on for some time got louder, and I got up to answer the door, but no one was there. The pounding came again, from somewhere over our heads, definitely inside the building. "Jeannie, get out here," I said. "Someone's doing something. Something's happening."

"It almost sounds like it's coming from your place, doesn't it?" she said. She came through, not fierce at all but oddly languid, blowing smoke at the aquarium. The knocks stopped. "I'll go up there and check," she said.

"Don't leave me here alone," I said. "I'm serious."

"Here, give me your key," she said, talking as one would to a child.

I locked the door behind her and went to wait by the window, craning my neck to see if someone who wanted to kill us was pressed up against the building, but all I saw was the empty, darkening view down the street. Two old men were attempting to wheel themselves out of the nursing home at the end of the block, ignored by a group of nurses laughing and smoking cigarettes under the security light. I saw this all the time, had called to complain about it, and I wondered if Borden ever watched it; through this window he had the exact same view I did. The glass was greaseless, spotless. I imagined what our two faces must look like from the outside, one on top of the other, peering through our windows with the blank, identical expressions of passengers on a train. The other units in the fourplex faced north, looked out over a frontage road that led to a mall, though the tenants on that side of the building changed frequently and weren't around much while they did live there: young couples getting through the winter before they got married, attractive divorcees getting back on their feet, graduate students finishing up their dissertations. I never noticed any of them looking out their windows.

I waited, watching the nursing home and listening to Borden's messages; four more financial advisors called, and then a woman who had to be Frieda came on, though her voice was more formal and youthful than I had imagined. "I never know what to say on these machines," she said. "I hope you're having a lovely time, you deserve it, Tom. Well, I thought it would be nice for you to have a message when you get home. I'll sign off now. Have a lovely vacation." The click and silence after her call filled me with sadness: poor Frieda had been left behind, the way we were all going to be left behind, only in her case it was worse because she probably loved Borden, in her own drab, faded way. *Goddamn Jeannie,* I thought, as though she had something to do with it.

Upstairs, the energy of real fear surprised me. My apartment's door was unlocked and I let myself in, trying to comprehend that something terrible, life-changing, could be waiting, just moments ahead of me in time. I stalled there by the door, switching my three-way lamp twice through bright, brighter, brightest, and then Jeannie padded in, blinking and nude, her skinny body, tiny breasts exactly the same as they'd been in sixth grade. For a second I thought *rape, hostage, help,* but then I saw her expression and something deflated in my chest. "Bachelor party hijinks," she said.

"Hey!" the professor called from my bedroom in his proper, lecture-hall voice. "Is that CeCe? CeCe, come in here! CeCe, I want to say hello!"

"You were in my *bed?*" I said.

"This wasn't my idea, honest," Jeannie said. "I didn't even know it was him until I got up here."

"CeCe! CeCe!" Roger called. He said my name like it was hypothetical, a joke.

Jeannie stepped up and tried to hug me. "Just ignore him," she said. "They were drinking Rumpelmints. He thought we were at your place. He tried to beep me but my battery was dead." I tried to push her away, but she got her skinny arms over my shoulders, her chin against my ear. "It's okay," she said, her oniony mouth warm against my cheek. "Nothing is going to change, we'll see each other all the time, nothing will be any different."

"Jesus, you have a beeper?" I said. I couldn't get her arms unlocked from around me.

"CeCe!" Roger shouted. "Let me see those boots of yours! I wish Jeannie would get some of those!"

"Don't worry, don't worry," Jeannie was whispering, only it was no longer Jeannie, and no longer me. I shut my eyes and put my hands on her bare back, hypothetically, feeling her ribs, her smooth sides and small breasts, her onion breath in my hair, and I thought, *This is what Roger does, this is what he gets,* and I tried to imagine what kind of luck he thought he had, getting this. It no longer had anything to do with me. Then I imagined Borden imagining this, sitting by the window wanting this, at the expense of poor, polite Frieda. And who could blame him? Everyone wanted it. I pushed Jeannie hard and she stepped back.

"*What,*" she said. "What is your problem? Is it the lottery? Any of us could have won the lottery."

"Do whatever you want," I said. "I'm going back down to Borden's." *Prostitute.* She followed me out into the hall and stood there naked, blabbing away like an anchorwoman.

"CeCe, nothing substantial has changed since yesterday, or the day before that, or the day before that," she was saying. "You are creating a self-fulfilling prophecy!" "Fine, good," I heard her say, when she thought I was finally out of her range.

• • •

In a dream the sailor came back to me. We sat side by side on a dock overlooking some calm water, and he helped me put back together the pieces of a paper horse I had accidentally torn up. The pieces of the horse were small and he took them in his hands with great tenderness. I turned to look at him, filled with feeling, and the gold buttons on his uniform caught the sun, blinding me. Through the explosion of light I reached for him, unable to see my own fingers, and then the spaghetti smell was there, as close as my own mouth. It was Borden, his face right there, the lamp switched on behind him, and I pushed back at him frantically. "Hey, pussycat, pussycat, take it easy," he said. He was sitting against my hip, pressing me into the back of his sofa, grinning down at me with gray teeth. Chest hair bloomed in a small bouquet from under the neckline of his T-shirt. "Don't touch me," I managed to say.

"Hey, okay," he said, raising his hands as though I'd pointed a gun at him. He stood and shuffled off toward the kitchen, his thighs whiffing against each other. "Jeez, I *live* here," he said.

"What are you doing here?" I said. It was late, three or four, and Borden's living room seemed calm, even peaceful, the mollies moving slowly up and down in their tank. I pulled myself into a sitting position and looked around for my boots.

"Well, it's funny," he said. "I had a funny feeling. I got all the way over to Epcot, got in my room, got one of them minirefrigerators with one of everything and then some other stuff you get free, fruit and that, and then I go take a look out the window and that big goddam *ball* is sitting there. It don't do nothing, you know? It don't rotate, don't open up, don't take off, nothing. Gave me a bad feeling, just knowing it was out there. And then my legs was acting up, you ever hear of restless legs syndrome? Secretaries get it, from all that sitting, you might know. It's when your legs, at night, try to do all the running you was supposed to do during the day but you didn't. Anyway, here I am. How about that, you think I'm crazy?" He stood in front of the open refrigerator, the cold, colorful food steaming behind him.

"You went to Epcot?" I said.

"Yeah. Where was I supposed to go? Hey, you don't have to leave or nothing," he said.

"I've got to get going," I said.

"Say, where's your girlfriend at? Ain't that her car out front?"

Our family's poodle had died like this, when I was a child: she ran out onto the two-lane highway, then froze on the center line when she saw the traffic coming. It was impossible for her to go forward and impossible to go back. She stood there in the wind of rushing cars, turning her curly, quivering head back and forth, looking one way, then the other, until a truck finally clipped her, knocking her sideways into the eastbound lane, where a Chevy got her.

"I can't go up there," I said.

"Jeannie's up at your place? Well, tell her to come on down and join the party."

"*Borden*," I said.

"Hey, hey, what's the matter?" He came back over to the sofa and sat, reaching down and lifting my legs by the ankles, before I could stop him, so that my feet rested in his lap. Once they were there, I thought it would be cruel to yank them off; I didn't want to hurt his feelings. His big thighs felt synthetic, slippery and impersonal as upholstery against my bare heels, and I imagined Jeannie watching from the doorway, the little sarcastic points of her eyes and mouth and naked breasts. "I'll tell you what," Borden said. "You're okay, CeCe. At least you got some integrity, some principles. You're the first one so far who ain't tried to get some of the prize for yourself. How about that? You thought I was too big and fat for you before and now that I got the cash, I'm still too big and fat. What do you know?"

"Hello, Tom, it's me again." He gazed, confused, at the wall telephone instead of at the whirring machine, where the woman's voice was coming from. "I don't want to use up your tape over nothing, but you won't believe what just happened to me. I was coming out of Winn-Dixie . . ."

"I was just at Winn-Dixie!" Borden said.

"She can't hear you, why don't you . . ."

"Shh," he said.

". . . out of collins mix, but I only had *one,* I said it before I went out, I said, 'Frieda, tonight you will behave like a *lady.*' So I told the officer I was celebrating for you, I said, 'Officer, I am not in my normal mode,' but he didn't even believe I know you! He said, 'Right, lady,' and then he grabs my arm real hard, and I told him, 'Don't you put your hands on me! When I *tell* you to put your hands on me, you do so with gusto, but when I *say,*' and he says, 'Oh, the lady's got rules!'" She paused, swallowing, and the machine cut her off.

"You can pick up the phone while she's talking," I told Borden, but he just sighed, his thighs giving a little under my feet as though some of the air had gone out of them.

"I know I'm supposed to be celebrating," he said, "but man, everybody *wants* something, you know?"

"Not Frieda," I said.

"What do you know about Frieda?" Borden said. He dug his thumb into the soft ball of my foot and I tried to jerk it away from him, but the cushions under me were soft and I couldn't get any leverage. "A Chinese girl did this to me one time," Borden said. "Something-su, I forget what it's called. You'll like it."

"*Please* quit that," I said. "All I meant was, Frieda seems to respect and depend on you."

"Naw, she don't love me. She just wants attention, you know? Her old man's in jail, over in Starke, HRS got her kids, and she ain't even allowed in half the bars in the county, because she's always looking at someone's husband and licking her straw. I seen her get a black eye for doing that. That's why she comes by here, because she don't got nowhere else to go, you know what I'm saying?"

"I don't want to know about Frieda," I said. "Maybe she likes her life, maybe she likes not having any responsibility, not having to worry about anything . . ."

"Naw, she don't," Borden said. "No one wants everything taken from them. Everyone wants some give." Frieda had come back on, meanwhile, saying something about Weight Watchers, but Borden spoke right over her—rudely, I thought, even if she did want something from him. "You want to hear something nuts?" he said. "When I got this thing confirmed, that I really hit it big, what's the first thing popped into my head? *Breeder tank.* Number one, my breeding females been dying, I gotta get some more, and a breeder tank. Number two, this tie I saw on TV, one of them shopping shows, some kind of a silk *weave.* I mean, does a Porsche occur to me? No. Yacht? No. Paris, France? Forget it. Girl I took out in high school whose old man was a commie, he was always asking me what was my *ambition,* because he *knew.* He knew I didn't have none. He told me, he said, 'This is how they keep you down—whatever you got, you think that's all you deserve.' You get so you only see one inch in front of your own face, he said."

"Well, what *are* you going to do?" I said.

Borden took his damp hands off my feet and pressed them over his eyes, then combed them back through his thin hair over and over again. He stared across the room at the hovering mollies. "You know what?" he finally said. "I just want to think about it tomorrow."

"Borden, I need to ask you a favor," I said. "Only certain things need to be clear up front. It's not money or anything . . ."

"You can stay here, just go on back to sleep, don't worry about it," he said, before I could go on. He stood up and walked with his hands in his pockets over to the window. "Don't worry about me," he said. He cupped his hands like blinders against the glass to block out the reflection of the lamp and sighed, making a small patch of steam. "I'm a perfect gentleman," he said.

• • •

In the morning he was gone. A note taped on the aquarium glass said: *I went back to You Know Where. I don't want to disturb your beauty sleep. Please feed the fish, O.K.?* I found my boots in the kitchen and left, shutting the door quickly and quietly, as though someone were still in the apartment, sleeping.

I got Jeannie out of my bed and we sat at my kitchen table, smoking cigarettes over plates of eggs. The professor had left right after I'd gone back downstairs to Borden's, she said. She suggested we spend the day together, go to a street fair or maybe go see the royal stallions that walked around on their hind legs. "Or how about that Wet Water place you applied at?" she said.

"We're too old for that shit," I said. "People have heart attacks there."

"Well, I'm paying," she said, "so decide."

At the dog track, where we ended up, she bought me some popcorn and then ran off to the clubhouse to say hello to a jai-alai player she knew. I stayed in the stands, trying to understand the loud announcer, the endless blur of greyhounds whipping by behind their strange fuzzy lure, but after Jeannie had been gone a while I gave up and stared at the crowd instead. An unexpected hot wind had come up off the Gulf, and people were sitting on their wadded-up jackets and mopping their foreheads with concession napkins. So many of them resembled Borden, I thought— so many lumpy bodies and damp, hungry-looking faces. Right in front of me a man who could have been Borden had stood up and was unzipping and peeling off one sweatshirt after another like a birthday party magician pulling scarves out of a sleeve. Maybe it was an effect of the sun, or the pony sofa smell steaming off my hair, but each time he got another sweatshirt off and revealed yet another one underneath, my scalp prickled with anticipation, as though we were all there to bet on sweatshirts instead of dogs. I thought of the real Borden wistfully, as though it had been a long time since we had seen each other, and I wished he were there with me, watching; I imagined his damp, gentlemanly face happy for once, laughing, finally, at his own good fortune.

guest speaker

The guest speaker flies in on the last day of July, and you are there to meet him. You watch the speck of his plane approach from behind the terminal's glass wall, which boils against the palm of your hand as though an invisible fire rages just outside. The sun is so powerful you can see through your thumb, which looks old, though you are young. The jet taxis hugely in, sending its thrilling, screaming roar up through the carpet. When you're in your windowless office, only a few miles from here, typing memos for Dr. Mime, you never, ever think about this airport, the people strolling through it, the woods and swamps spread out around it, or the enormous blue sky. A massive wooden octagon a few feet from you houses four TVs, each facing in a different direction, each showing Oprah Winfrey, whose upbeat, reproachful gaze addresses those who have not taken sufficient charge of their lives. A woman in Oprah's audience yells, "Honey, if he did it to me, he's gonna do it to you!" You put your hand on your shoulder bag, feeling the hard shape of the stolen tape recorder through the corduroy. Actually, it is not exactly stolen, but you cannot help but feel like a criminal. It is an old feeling, the feeling that you are trying to get away with something, something for which you will surely be forced to pay, eventually, though in this case you don't even have a plan, you're not even sure what you're trying to get away with.

The recorder is Dr. Mime's; he speaks into it as though he is a secret agent, holding his lips and teeth still so that you cannot make out certain words and have to type blank lines in their place, as he has instructed you to do in such an instance. *Cliff and Linda need to help me find my _____ that I misplaced the middle of last week,* you type. My garden? My bargain? My Darlene? It is impossible to tell. *To ask Williamson: Were we interested in whether anyone's been looking at the litigation papers that are filed with _____?* He uses surveillance equipment on you as well: cameras in the corridors, a computer that keeps track of your phone calls, who knows what else? He sucks Tic-Tacs all day long, keeps cartons of them in your office's file cabinet—you can even hear them clicking against his teeth on the memo tapes—but he never offers a single Tic-Tac to you or anyone. And although he owns two or three Cessnas, his hobby, he never offers to take anyone for a ride, though he makes the mailroom guy hose down the planes on days like Veterans Day, when there is work but no mail. You yourself have tutored little dyslexic Barry Mime in fractions, though you are a part-time employee, no benefits, and Nancy, a customer service operator, always takes the Mime Mercedeses in for their emissions tests. And now it's your job to chauffeur the guest speaker, who will speak at an executive function to which you are not invited.

To all employees, night custodial staff NOT *excluded,* you typed, earlier this week. *Topic: Suspicious individuals in your neighborhood making inquiries of you or your family regarding MimeCo or Dr. Mime. Last night a suspicious individual was making inquiries regarding me at the residences of my neighbors. This is possibly* related to the controversial nature of our upcoming visiting guest speaker. Naturally, I followed up as appropriate. If such an individual contacts you by telephone or in person, it would be helpful if you could tell them, "I don't have time to talk now, but please call me or return tomorrow at this same time." Thank you for your assistance in this matter. This is the unfortunate side of business and we are going to pursue it in a _____ fashion. Richard fashion? Bitchier fashion? Denatured fashion? *Mature*, that was it, you typed it in— and then, without even thinking about it, you switched off the recorder and dropped it into your bag, which sat slumped between your ankles on the floor. When Linda came to the doorway of your office a minute later, your stomach turned over.

"You are *red*," she said. Linda sells Mary Kay and always comments on your appearance, pushing you to let her give you a makeover, but even thinking about confronting your face matter-of-factly like that causes you shame. You purse your lips and duck your head whenever you have to look into a mirror, hanging on to certain illusions. You cry at night, sometimes, like anyone: *Oh God, oh God, I'm so lonely, I'm so lonely.*

"Coffee makes me flush," you told her.

She gave you a look that said, "You are crazy." Sometimes she just says it aloud to you, so you know the look. "Well, hand it over," she said then.

You just looked at her.

"Your *time card*," she said. "Girl, wake up! It's Friday!"

After she walked away you felt the sharp edge of the recorder with your instep, and then you cut it out of your thoughts altogether, as though Mime's clocks and cameras and computers might pick up its presence there.

Driving home you had an itchy scalp, a sign of guilt, your mother would have said, and in fact you also had the sinking sense of inevitable wrongness that you'd always felt around your mother. When you were a child your toys would disappear if you left them lying around on cleaning day; if you asked when you would get them back, she would say, "When I feel like it."

Sometimes when she was out you would visit your Dawn doll in her bottom dresser drawer, but there would have been no pleasure in taking it out and playing with it. And there was a moment that came right after the first chorus of "Killing Me Softly," a record you'd won at a birthday party, that made your heart jump for years whenever you heard it, ever since the day your mother shouted your name at that moment in the song because she'd just discovered something else you'd done wrong, something you'd thought you'd gotten away with but which she had just then discovered.

But your mother was, or claimed to be, an unhappy woman, and when you complained as a teenager about how cold she had been, how cruel, she argued that it was only because she felt things so much more deeply than others. "Every morning I used to zip you into your parka and kiss you goodbye," she said, "but then one day when you were in second grade you pushed me away and told me not to kiss you, and I felt so hurt, so rejected, that I never tried to kiss you again—what else could I have done?" No warmth blossomed between the two of you after that explanation, but at least she had offered one. Mime does not seem to feel that he needs any, and perhaps he doesn't, being only a boss and not a mother.

The guest speaker pushes through the turnstile. In person he barely resembles his book jacket photo; he does not appear to be brooding or contemplating danger and loss. His head seems smaller. He wears dark woolen clothes, inappropriate in the heat, and his hand is delicate, scrubbed and vulnerable-looking on the strap of his carry-on bag. You step forward to introduce yourself and, without planning it or even knowing you're going to do it, you use a fake name. "I'm Alex Trotter," you say. Alex Trotter is a boy you slept with a few times in college, just after your mother's death—he is, actually, the last boy you slept with. That was two years ago, and his name bursts out of your mouth as though of its own volition, as though it has waited long enough.

The guest speaker smiles photogenically and says, "Alex," and you feel a little dizzied. A memory shoots back to you: when you were seven or eight, just after your father left you and your mother for his girlfriend in Norway, your mother explained to you that in real life princesses did not wear fancy gowns, were not necessarily pretty (Look at Margaret and Anne, she said, who were *homely*)—princesses looked, she said, like anyone, like everyone. The next morning, without planning it, you told the other children on the bus to school that you were a princess, explaining in the commanding, reasonable tones of your mother that there was no way of knowing a princess by her appearance alone. It was not exactly a lie; if there was no way of knowing, weren't you as much a princess as a princess nobody knew was one? And though you remember almost nothing firsthand about your father—just the outlines of his kind blond face, his low voice singing "Mares eat oats and does eat oats and little lambs eat ivy," him pressing his handkerchief to your face, saying, "You have a booby in your nose"—you remember the moment after your princess lie as perfectly as though it happened yesterday: you gazed out the smudgy bus window, changed and desperate and ordinary all at once.

"I'm all yours, Alex," the guest speaker says. His smallness suddenly seems calculated, fierce, like that of a ferret. He writes about outrages in other countries, chemical leaks and medical scams and robber barons—"America's angriest writer," a blurb on one of his book jackets says. His wife has the name of some foreign, toxic flower; you read it in the dedication of his first book and thought, *Of course, how perfect.*

In the front seat of your mother's old Fury the guest speaker asks polite questions about the town. You answer a few truthfully—"I can drive from one end to the other in eighteen minutes," you tell him—but then you begin to make things up or steal information from the lives of your friends, who are mostly secretaries or assistants like yourself. You invent and describe ordinary pets and relatives, small adventures and ambitions and defeats. You have two hamsters, Hanky and Panky, you say, and one time you found Siamese twin baby turtles in your backyard; they could only walk in a circle and you named them Yin and Yang. You tell him your mother is still alive, is in fact the most popular dentist in the county, the only female dentist, too, and you mention that you heard that in Japan it only costs fourteen dollars to get a root canal. While you talk, you notice in the rearview that the couple in the car behind yours is having an animated conversation in sign language, and for a moment it seems that you too are making shapes in the air with your words, producing and erasing commonplace things like a magician manipulating scarves and coins and wristwatches. The silver windows of the Hilton flash just off the highway, but you whiz past. "Room's not ready yet," you lie.

"That's all right," the guest speaker says. "I'm on vacation. Why don't you be my guide, show me what you do for fun?"

You smile in a measured way so that he not recognize how easily charmed you are. For fun you order Szechuan beef sometimes. You have accepted without complaint or question, though you hadn't realized you accepted it until this moment, the absence of men attempting to charm you. But *why*? you wonder now. You feel anxious, like a guest arriving at a fabulous party several hours late—what will be left for you? "There's a bar I once went to over on the Panhandle," you tell him. This happens to be the truth. It is the only excursion out of town you have taken since your mother died—you met with your mother's lawyer, signed papers, turned down his offer of dinner, and drank one gin and tonic alone at this bar. "They were so drunk and Southern there I could barely understand a word they said," you say. "This man with a sunken-in face came up to me and said something that sounded like 'Flip knot' over and over. Then he went back to his stool and said, 'If you see something you want, go for it,' until the barmaid yelled at him and kicked him out the door."

"Perfect," the guest speaker says. "Love it."

A moment later, he says, "So what do you think of human blood and suffering? Ever seen any?"

"What?" you say.

"Do you ever feel removed from it?" he says. "You know, being alive and all?"

You glance at him, but he looks like anyone, like everyone—there is no way of knowing a madman by his appearance alone. In his last book, titled *Uh-Oh*, he wrote about some children in Brazil who found glowing radioactive powder in a public dump and smeared it all over their faces, playing clowns and phantoms. How angry is he, exactly? you wonder. You think of the suspicious individuals making inquiries, you picture the guest speaker's graceful angry hands around your throat. Traffic veers off an exit behind you as you speed recklessly ahead; the deaf couple—if they even *were* deaf—have vanished. Humdrum moments from your recent life crowd you, demanding payback. *My God*, you think, *if I live through this, I must get busy.*

But then he is unwrapping a stick of gum for you and apologizing. "I'm uncouth," he is saying. He is charming again. You take the gum, and a deep breath. "I am highly visible," he says. "I have a wife, children. But that's all on the outside, you know what I mean?"

He is speaking again in sensible cliché, and you nod with relief, feeling your hair swing, the pretty hair of Alex Trotter. The real Alex was not kind. He asked, a day or two after your mother died, what you planned to do with your life, and when you told him that you had no idea, he said, "Well, get cracking." His tone of voice reminded you of the way your mother would stand on the porch, holding open the screen door, waiting for the cat to decide whether or not it wanted to go out, saying, "Would you make up your alleged mind?"

"I'm forty," the guest speaker says, "and I've been all over the world, but I've never been in the hospital, never been to a funeral. Have you been to a funeral?"

"Yes," you say, "but it didn't seem real. It didn't make anything seem any more real. Isn't that what funerals are supposed to do?" You borrowed eyeliner from one of your mother's friends in the funeral home's rest room after the burial. Two chigger bites on your ankle itched furiously all through the service. The next day you bought a can of apple juice from the machine in your dormitory's lobby, a can that had probably been placed in the machine before your mother's death. Everything seemed impartial, improbable. "There was no human blood," you tell the guest speaker.

He laughs. "You seem like a tough girl, Alex," he says. "Do you want to wallow with me?"

"Maybe," you say, smiling your new, offhand smile, Alex's smile. And maybe you do. Maybe this is the opportunity you've been waiting for. Go for it, you imagine your sexy blond father saying, though you know he is no longer blond, sexy, or even in Norway. You want for a moment to tell the guest speaker your real name, the real facts of your life, but, you rationalize, if what you are covering up is nothing of worth, nothing of much substance or purpose, you're not really lying, are you?

• • •

Perhaps you know the story of the hundred-year-old woman and the ice cream, your father wrote to you one summer. *The woman was asked what she would do differently if she could live her life over again, and she said, "Smell more wildflowers, and eat more ice cream." The point is that if you go through life lying to please others, you are giving nothing to them or yourself. And if you lie to please yourself, the best you will ever have to call your own is a moment. You might as well be a ghost: you will move through the world, but you won't be living. These are important principles and you are not too young to understand them.*

You were fourteen and had just come home from the beach. Your friends Tutti and Chrissy were with you, and all three of you were excited because at the beach you had met some long-haired older boys who told you they were the members of Cheap Trick. The boys had stood in the surf a little farther in than you, grinning and beckoning, flexing their skinny chests, the waves darkening their cutoffs, and you and Tutti and Chrissy had come close to them, but not too close. You high-stepped through the rising and falling water, scared of stepping on a crab, not wanting to get too wet, picking at your bikini bottom and your hair. The conversation was not about whether they were telling the truth, as it would have been if you were all boys, but about whether or not you believed them. "I would *know*," you told the boys, but you didn't want to know, and it was not required of you to decide one way or another, since of course once you decided there would be nothing to talk about. This went on for hours.

The dim beige hush of your living room afterwards was stifling, but then you saw the letter, unopened, on the floor beneath the mail slot, and your face burned as though the sun, the boys, had sneaked in after you. You bent over to pick it up and your heart rushed as though you were stealing something. Your mother was still at work. "Who do *you* know in another country?" Tutti asked, and you said, "A guy," and would tell them no more.

When your mother came home, however, you did not bother to remove the letter from the hassock on which you'd left it. She had given you permission so many times to keep secret your correspondence with your father—"or anything else you feel should be private," she often added—that there was no point. He had only sent two or three letters, total, and never one like this—seven handwritten pages from a full-sized legal pad, talking about life and your mother and happiness—but after Tutti and Chrissy left you could not escape an odd sense of letdown, and the last thing you felt like doing was reading it, or writing a letter back. What you wanted to do, and what you did, was to lie on your bed in the dark late, late into the night and imagine again the boys on the beach.

• • •

You take one of the county road exits and angle the creaking car onto a dirt turnoff that heads into plantings of young pine. A bleached wooden sign at the road's entrance says SNACKS—1/4 MILE; otherwise, you have no idea what to expect. You have never been out this way. A breeze through the open passenger window brings you a whiff of strong pine and the guest speaker's insidious cologne, probably purchased for him by his wife. You bump along in silence, taking little sips of the disturbing scent, until the road finally opens onto a dirt and gravel clearing containing two metal-sided sheds. One is set back in the high weeds and is the size of a doghouse or bathroom. The other has a door that looks like it's woven of chicken wire, propped open against the back of a large, napping goat. The guest speaker says, "I love that." You step over the goat, your heart pounding.

Inside are two short old women in jeans and flannel shirts and tractor caps, and, miraculously, the man with the sunken face. They are all sitting at a flimsy-looking, vinyl-topped card table, smoking cigarettes and drinking beer out of juice glasses. "You got to have that little flip, or your goddamn trowel sticks," one of the women is saying. A cartoon of a locomotive bouncing out of control down the side of a mountain flickers on a small soundless TV on the bar, and a busy munching noise comes from behind the counter, down near the cement floor. You see the black and white hoof of another goat, like something on a keychain, poking out beside the leg of the bar stool on the end. "You looking for the sink?" the old woman talking about bricklaying says, and the sunken-faced man says, "Where you from, baby?"

"The bathroom?" you say.

"The *sinkhole*," says the old woman. "Fifty yards down the path. You pay here."

"Hey, where you from?" the sunken-faced man says again.

"How much?" the guest speaker asks the woman.

"Two dollars apiece," she says.

"What's down there?" he asks.

"Well now, you got to pay to see," she says.

The sunken-faced man stands and strolls over to you. He stops when his collapsing face is just inches from yours, the yellow whites of his eyes gleaming beneath pale irises. "You know where you're from?" he says.

"Yes," you say. He can't possibly know your name; you're sure you never told it to him on the Panhandle.

"You're from your *mama*," he says. "You're from your *mama*."

"Thank you kindly," the old woman says to the guest speaker, taking his money. They are smiling at each other like friends.

Gnats fly into your mouth as you and the guest speaker follow the path through the brush. The goat from the doorway has waked up and is trotting a few feet behind you, making worried human sounds. Every time you turn to look at it, it stops and turns its long, sad face away, as though embarrassed. At the end of the path the ground dips and runs into the very round, very dark pond, which looks hundreds of feet deep. Moss hangs from the cypress, breaking up the glare and shading a line of seven sleeping turtles at the water's edge. "Ah," says the guest speaker. His small hands move down his shirt, unbuttoning.

"I'll go back and get us some beers," you say, blushing. He just laughs. You turn your back and hear, rather than see, his splash. Back in the little bar you interrupt the women again. "You can only do it two ways, honest or dishonest," one of them is saying. "You turn your hand, bring it down the line, and it's boogety, boogety, all fun and games." The other woman nods with satisfaction before they turn to you to see what you want.

The sunken-faced man never looks up from his glass, just stares down into it, shaking his head as though agreeing with something.

When you return, the guest speaker is floating on his back in a patch of sun, his eyes closed. His boxer shorts balloon up around his legs like a tiny life raft. The goat is kneeling shyly beside the dozing turtles, nibbling sand. You wedge the cans of beer in the ground and roll down your panty hose, feeling ridiculous. It seems there should be a way for you to skip from dressed to undressed, traversing shame and fumbling and uncertainty, but there isn't. At the last moment, you reach in your bag and turn on the tape recorder, thinking, *This is the part I want to remember*. Of course, there is no way the little machine will be able to record the two of you at such a distance, through corduroy. But you do it anyway. You are naked, but there are still things he doesn't see, doesn't know.

The solid cold of the water is shocking. Treading, you feel split in two, your scalp dry and burning and exposed, your body lost in the slow, deep cold. You try to relax, but beneath the surface you feel both invisible and vulnerable, almost itchy. You are afraid of little, sinister things: worms and weeds and biting fish, all of which are down there, sensing you in ways over which you have no control. *Let me out*, your twitching body seems to say, but the guest speaker says, "Come over here." Stuck to his cheek is the wing of some large insect, a lacy oval that looks like a third eye, a ghost eye. You paddle closer, and as you do you notice for the first time how blue his real eyes are, as bright and deep as the springs. They are real, but they don't look real. "Are you wearing colored contact lenses?" you ask.

He smiles his slow, remorseless smile. "No," he says. "I'm just beautiful."

"Oh," you gasp. You cannot shake this coldness, this strange invisibility. Your body lists toward his, desire hurtling through you. But you wonder, *Will I even feel it, if he touches me in this cold? And, if I can't feel it, is it really happening?*

• • •

"You know, even if your mother were still alive," Alex Trotter once remarked, "she couldn't tell you what it is you want. You'd still have to figure that out on your own." He was sitting at his computer, his back to you, programming his resumé into a mail merge. It had been ten, eleven days since the funeral. "Even your perfect daddy couldn't do that for you," he said. His fingers never stopped moving, tap-tapping the keys.

"Why are you saying these things?" you said, your face growing numb.

Alex's fingers paused and he turned his head halfway. You noticed the stack of wrinkles that formed in the back of his neck; they reminded you of TV MagicCards, the man who did the tricks in the commercial, so many years ago. "I'm only saying one thing," he said, "and I say it because I care: Whatever you're doing five years from now, you'll have no one but yourself to thank or blame. That's all I have to say."

You stood and walked down the hall to his clean kitchen and opened his cabinet and got down a package of Hydrox cookies. You ate two quickly and dropped one on the floor, crushing it to powder with your boot heel before you went out the back door. The tap-tapping went on and on. "Goodbye," you called, when you knew you were too far away for him to hear.

What kind of a favor had he thought he was doing for you? *Advice has nothing to do with reality*, your mother sometimes said. *Live your life.* But maybe that was just another way of saying what Alex was saying; maybe she and Alex were not so far apart in their views, after all. In the hospital, even, after her heart attack, she was efficient. *Get my purse*, she said, and *You know which drawer I'm talking about, right?* The last thing she said to you was, sensibly, "Good night."

When she died, your father contacted you for the first time in years, a flowered card among other flowered cards, containing, as the others did, phone numbers. He also enclosed a photo of himself and his family: not an action shot, a team of glamorous blondes caught by the camera in the midst of their whirling pursuit of wildflowers and happiness, but four stocky, sweatered people set up against a false cornfield backdrop. On the back of the photo, in a confident, ballooning hand, was written, "Please phone us!" There has been no shortage, these past two years, of people offering you sensible solace, guidance through the real world. And, really, Alex was right: you can't blame any of them for whatever it is you are missing now. It is not as though you ever thought to ask any of them—your mother, your father, Alex, Dr. Mime, Tutti, Chrissy, or anyone—why it was, in *their* opinion, that people bothered to go on living.

• • •

Monday morning you walk through the shimmering glass and leather lobby of MimeCo with the gait of a ghost or movie star. Your forearms, face, and scalp are sunburned, but the sting, disappointingly, is already gone; you keep touching the part in your hair to make sure. The chigger bites you had on your ankle at your mother's funeral continued to itch for a week—whenever you had a chance that week you examined, picked, and scratched them, dabbed them with witch hazel, pulled off their scabs. When they finally faded you had the oddest feeling, as though they had deserted you.

Two silent, newspaper-clutching men from the promotion department step into the elevator beside you. As the heavy door hisses shut, you notice the lit panel of buttons—someone has pressed them all. One of the men says, "Crap," and shakes his head. The other, who is shorter than you are and has bad acne, kicks the wall of the elevator with the toe of his loafer and says, "Whoever done that's an idiot." Neither man glances your way.

After the men get off, you go seven more floors, standing as though hypnotized through the rising and stopping, opening and shutting. You keep remembering something, playing it over and over in your head—not anything as real or definite as the guest speaker's sharp, handsome face, but just a moment, a split second in the cool, conditioned dark of his hotel room, before you changed your mind and put on your clothes and went home. All you could see was the blackness, when against your neck he said softly what he thought was your name: *Alex.* You almost said *What?* but then you caught yourself, caught your breath, because he wasn't going to tell you anything, he was simply speaking out loud what he thought was your name. And at that moment you realized you had made the leap, had swung over or past the wrong answer like a girl on a trapeze, that you were not even required to answer, but only to listen to a man who desired you speak your name in the dark. You might not have even re-membered it but for the tape recorder, which picked up the word clearly, the first clear word in an hour of muffled rushing and bumping noises, faint, vaguely human sounds, like a record of poltergeists. You've erased the tape already, and the recorder's safe in your bag, ready to return, probably never missed. It may have been, as your father said, only a moment. But it is yours, yours.

dream, age twenty-eight

Though I'm an adult, I'm in the neatly kept bedroom of my childhood. Nothing has changed—the yellow plaster walls, the single bed with its orange poly-fill bedspread, the lifeless walnut-framed intercom that was built into the wall in the 1950s, before my family moved in. I've been away for many years, far from here and alone, building my life as one would a house, warily, feeling the weight of every brick, lifting and placing each one, seeing the shape of the house rise up in the air before it is visible, before it even exists.

Here, though, nothing has changed. Outside my bedroom door the argument is getting louder and faster, gathering heat, billowing out of control like a fire. My sister, thirty, still lives here, but she's telling my mother and father her plans to leave; she's going to be an actress, an actress, she cries, and they scream back at her, *Don't be ridiculous, you will never make it, never make it, you are living in a fantasy, a fantasy.* It is earsplitting, liable at any moment to burst through the hollow wood door and into my room, the shouting and running, the furious voices rising and bleating like the cries of animals, the quick heavy footsteps thumping past on the carpeted floorboards, back and forth, advancing and retreating, *I'm going to be an actress, an actress; You are nothing, nothing.* So fierce, so palpable is my mother's anger that I can almost see her through the wall, about to explode in my direction like a small violent man, her fury bigger than her small body, bigger than any of us, swelling and filling the house like smoke and blowing down all the doors. Gingerly, holding my breath so as not to make a sound, I lean over and with one finger press the button in the center of the gold doorknob. The button stays down. I wait. It takes all my concentration to keep her on the other side of that door.

After a while the noise subsides somewhat, the angry voices retreating back behind another door, though one pair of feet still goes slowly back and forth, back and forth, in the hallway outside my room. The feet stop and my doorknob rattles briefly, absently; then they move on. It is not my mother.

In the crack of space under the bottom of the door I see my sister's faded tan mules, their matted fleece, a sad, familiar sign of her disarray. I can picture the rest of her: her short, unwashed, unevenly cut hair, the chipped pink frost on her uneven nails, the worn yellow nightshirt with the peeling, cracking, nearly unrecognizable iron-on of a spotted horse standing on a little patch of ground. Even her step is unrealistic, uneven, irregular. It is as though I can hear the erratic whirring of her mind through the door. She wants to restate her case; if the door were open she wouldn't see me, really, or really know I'm here, she just wants to go over everything again, explain in rational terms her irrational plans, her fantasy, her passionate scenario. She will go to New York, persist long enough, and then make it. She has saved a couple of hundred dollars in her ceramic cocker spaniel bank. She has made tapes of herself singing Helen Reddy songs and reading dialogue on the GE tape recorder she received for her twelfth birthday. Elated, she will explain all of this, over and over, to my mother, my father, to me, to anyone who will listen. She must keep explaining, she wants to come in my room and keep explaining. I am relieved it is only her, not my mother, but still I don't let her in. I cannot afford to let her in.

Earlier, my parents asked her to audition for them. They were downstairs in the living room, my mother on the couch and my father in his recliner, my sister moving wildly, ungracefully, in the space before them. *Go ahead, show us*, my mother said, her voice heavy with sarcasm, with mockery, and my sister began to act out a scene from *The Wizard of Oz*, cackling in the high, fake voice of the Wicked Witch of the West, spitting out each word, pretending as fiercely as a child. *Oh, this is ridiculous*, my father said, and I could see him turn his head away in scorn and resignation, refusing to watch. *Keep going, we're waiting*, my mother said. My sister crouched and straightened, crouched and straightened, clenching her hands like claws around an imaginary broom, her eyes glassy, her face transported. *Jesus Christ*, my father said. I did not see any of this, but I could picture it well enough. I was upstairs in my room while it was happening, listening to all of it through the door.

Now I attempt to remove old newspaper clippings from the wall over my bed, razoring through brittle Scotch tape with my thumbnail, ripping the paper down and crumpling it in my fist. I stuck these things up there years ago: unfunny Garfield cartoons, photos of actors I loved from the TV page, ads for sandals and tube tops and lip gloss I coveted, items I believed would solve the problem of my body, my face, my life. I would not be ugly, a misfit, I would not be like my sister. The clippings do not come down easily, however. Some tear and come away from their strips of tape, others leave black lines of adhesive and newsprint on the plaster. Bits of tape and my own black fingerprints accumulate like storm clouds on the pale wall. My sister is gone from the hallway, my parents still shut up in their room discussing the situation, so I run down to the kitchen for a bottle of Windex, trying to move lightly, purposelessly, afraid my own fear and guilt will weigh my footsteps down, make them loud and heavy as thunder in the house. I make it, though, and back in my room I leave the door open, feigning nonchalance, invulnerability.

My sister arrives almost immediately. She comes out of her bedroom, a few feet down the hall from mine, pretending to be only casually strolling by this time, casually stopping. *Do you want to hear my new tape?* she says. *Mommy and Daddy won't listen but it's really good, I know I'm getting better.* She is smoking a cigarette, a Merit, but she is not inhaling, only holding it in a studied way between two fingers, putting it to her mouth and pursing her lips, blowing the invisible smoke away like a child.

I move my hands busily along the wall, picking at tape and keeping up my show of simple, constructive activity. *So I figure Greyhound is the cheapest,* she is saying. *You don't get any meals or anything, but I'm going to take some cheese and crackers and carrot sticks, so I really think it's worth it. I got some Baggies from downstairs, so I don't even have to pay for Baggies. I'm going to take some Kraft singles, too, because they're already past the expiration date, Mommy was going to throw them out this week anyway, there's no way she was going to use the whole package.*

While she has been talking I have reached the section of the wall on which the intercom is built, a dark brown square of shiny burlap framed in lighter brown. The two control knobs can be turned, but the speaker never crackles to life, and neither do the speakers in the other rooms. They only scowl darkly and uselessly on the walls, a testimonial to our family's peculiarity, for I have been to the houses of neighbors, of friends, and none of them have intercoms, not one. I notice the edge of a piece of tape sticking out just below the intercom, but when I try to peel it off my fingers hit something stiff and crinkly on the wall beneath the bottom edge of the speaker's frame. It is not a clipping but a wad of tape stuck there—no, not a wad, but a deliberate compartment, a small, many-layered cocoon. It comes right off in my hand, and I pick it apart like fruit.

Inside is a miraculous thing. It is money, a couple of dimes and one carefully rolled and folded bill which I can see is a large denomination even before I get it unrolled; the green curlicued design is different, unfamiliar, and a rush of excitement goes through my chest. *140.* I check twice but it's no mistake, the number printed in each corner is 140, it is a hundred-forty-dollar bill—rare and thrilling as an Indian-head penny, a buffalo nickel, a sudden visitation from another time. The memory tugs at me like an itch, like the place where a stain was on a shirt, like a memory of pain: the ghostly outline of myself, a young girl, taping the money to the wall. I can almost see it, almost remember. My ears must have buzzed, my spine locked as I stood there, my fingers fluttering like spiders beneath the frame, not knowing when it would be time, how much I would need when it was finally time to escape. The bill is crisp now in my hand, perfect, unsullied, still waiting. The years between then and now well up, so much hoarding, measuring, guarding—and are at last released, like a tremendous breath. *It's okay,* I cry across the years to her, *it's okay, I made it, you can stop worrying now.*

My sister's attention is on me suddenly, her eyes still blurry, unfocused, peering through the haze of her fantasy. She has stopped talking and is gazing at the money in my hands. *No, no way,* I think. *This is mine, it was always mine, both in the hiding and the finding; the fact that I didn't use it means it's even more mine, for when you don't need something, isn't that when you truly own it, instead of it owning you?*

It would help me, she says. *It would help me if you gave me that.* Or maybe she doesn't speak the words aloud. It is all around us in the air, coming from every cell of her, she wants the money.

No, no, I protest silently, but I must answer not only to her, no longer only to her. I apologize, but my apologies are hollow, false as my sister's fantasies, they are nothing. *Ten dollars,* I think desperately. *Fine, I'll give you ten bucks.* She goes away without comment and I'm left with the money, no longer pure. I hold the bill uncertainly, feeling its diminishment with my fingertips.

My father appears in the doorway next, angry about the mess I've made of the wall. Blue clouds of Windex I've sprayed and forgotten to wipe have stained the plaster, smearing the black gobs of adhesive and shredded paper there and dripping onto my bed. *Jesus*, my father says, and I jump to the mess before he can say anything else, making a show of purposeful though not panicky action. *It looks worse than it is*, I tell him, imitating tones of assurance, and he says, *Well you better get busy*, and I nod *Yes sir*, full of agreement, of sensible industry. I move quickly and try not to think too much, afraid that if I let it enter my mind he will perceive the money in my front jeans pocket, see it glowing there like something charged. He stands just inside the doorway, his hands in his own pockets, watching me scrub the wall with a paper towel in small, efficient circles. I don't glance back at him but after a while sense he is only half watching, half paying attention to my progress. Finally he gives a loud sigh, the last of his annoyance leaving him. *Well*, he says, sounding sheepish, as though he is granting me a great favor, *it's not such a big deal. Frankly, right now, we're a lot more worried about your sister.*

• • •

It is later the same day, almost sunset, and my sister has finally gone out to run some final errand before her trip. Everyone's door is open now. I move through the house in the fading light, feeling oddly weightless, the tension evaporated. A small transistor radio is still going in my sister's room, sending forth the miniature tinny voice of a weatherman. A storm is moving in from the east, he says. *Strange*, I think. Weather never comes in from the east.

My parents sit in their bedroom reading newspapers and keeping up a conversation, their tones smug, deliberately casual. *Now there's a good question*, my father says, loudly turning over a page. *Does 'child' have one syllable or two?* I walk by on my way to my sister's room, holding my breath in the second it takes to get past their doorway. *That's an oxymoron*, my mother is saying. *Grown-up child. I bet you didn't know that.*

Safely over the threshold, I let out my breath and shut the door. Clothes and wet towels, half-packed cardboard cartons torn and on their sides, half-eaten convenience store sandwiches and candy bar wrappers, soda cans and potato chip bags and used-up books of matches, half-smoked cigarettes and butts filling coffee cups and aluminum ashtrays—every surface is covered, the floor, the bed, the desk, the nightstand. This is how she has always kept it, this is the wreckage of my sister's room. And everywhere, everywhere, are ashes, gray mounds and smears and clumps rising like anthills, like natural formations in the mess, live embers still burning deep in some of them, threads of smoke snaking up into the air toward the benign face of the ceiling. Here and there on the mounds burn yellow flames the size of pinky fingernails. I spit on my own fingers and go around the room, tamping them out.

I've gotten most of them, stained my fingertips black with ashy slime, when I see the horse—a small white one the size of a cat, tied and standing calmly in a corner near the window. He is not dirty or skinny or sick-looking; he just stands there in a little cleared space, plump and white, turning his head and gazing around the smoky room as though waiting, looking for someone. *Oh*, I cry, moving to untie him. The small red halter is loose and I pull it easily over his head, and he steps back from me. *It's okay, baby*, I say, but he only stands there twitching his tail and looking idly around, unconcerned. I lean over his smooth back to open the window, let in some clean air. The late afternoon sky over our neighbor's patio is yellow and clear, the trees motionless, the fresh air cool and still, entering the room quietly through the window screen. *Are you hungry, are you thirsty?* I ask the horse, but he is oblivious, picking his way through the clutter, sniffing curiously at this and that. And he has not after all been abandoned, for my sister is still coming back, she hasn't yet left for good.

Still, I feel I must do something. *Hang on*, I tell him. *I'm going to get you something to eat.*

My mother and father glance up at me, amused and expectant, as I step into the hallway, into their view. I hold the door closed behind me so the horse won't get out. *You survived the disaster area*, my mother says dryly.

I'm just going to get some carrots, I say. *If that's okay. We have carrots, right?*

It'll take a lot more than carrots, my father says, and he and my mother both laugh, pleased with themselves.

There were actual fires burning, I tell them. I am nervous, afraid to let the conversation falter.

They look at each other, my father shaking his head. *How many times have we told her not to smoke in there?* he says.

She knows, my mother says. *She knows and she pays no attention, she's off in her own little dream world.* They look back at me as though expecting my contribution, my affirmation. This is crazy, I think. Have you forgotten already, forgotten that for so long, so many years, it was I who was the problem? They gaze at me with ironic half-smiles, not seeming to remember.

Well, I guess I'll go get some carrots, I say.

I open the door a crack and look back into my sister's room once more before going downstairs. The horse hears me but doesn't turn his head; he trots unhurriedly over to the window and stands there looking out at the yard, the sky. His eyes are dark, his expression calm and blank. My chest aches suddenly, terribly—*he is lonely! Of course*, I think, *horses are herd animals.* He stands breathing blankly, neither impatient nor patient, the object of his waiting murky, inarticulate, diffuse within his solid self. He does not yet know what it is he wants. But it is so clear to me, I can hardly stand it, my heart rushes all around—there must be something I can do! He is a herd animal! He stands there, the light in his face, watching, waiting . . .

• • •

But there was nothing I could do, I had to go ahead and shut the door. I could not then and cannot now do anything to make the situation right.

i am the bear

I said: Oh, for God's sake, I'm not some pervert—you think I'm like that hockey puck in New Jersey, the mascot who got arrested for grabbing girl's breasts with his big leather mitt at home games? I'm a polar bear! I molest no one, I give out ice cream cones in the freezer aisle, I make six dollars an hour, I majored in Humanities, I'm a *girl*.

I was talking to the Winn-Dixie manager in his office. Like every grocery-store manager, he had a pudgy face, small mustache, and worried expression, and he was trying very hard, in his red vest and string tie, to appear open-minded. He had just showed me the model's letter of complaint, which sat, now, between us, on his desk. *The polar bear gave me a funny feeling*, the model had written; *I was under the mistaken impression that the bear was male, but much to my surprise it turned out that I was wrong. The bear was silent the whole time and never bothered to correct me.*

It was part of my *job* not to talk, I explained to the manager. I read to him from my Xeroxed rules sheet: *Animal representatives must not speak in a human manner but should maintain animal behavior and gestures at all times while in costume. Neither encourage nor dispel assumptions made regarding gender.* I said, See? I was holding my heavy white head like a motorcycle helmet in the folds of my lap, my own head sticking out of the bureau-sized shoulders, my bangs stuck to my forehead, a small, cross-shaped imprint on the tip of my nose from the painted wire screen nostril of the bear. I can't help my large stature, I told him. That's why they made me a bear and not one of those squirrels who gives away cereal. I was doing exactly what I was supposed to do. I was doing what I was designed to do.

She would like an apology, the manager said.

You say one becomes evil when one leaves the herd; I say that depends entirely on what the herd is doing, I told him.

Look, the manager said, his eyes shifting. Would you be willing to apologize? Yes or no. He reminded me of a guy I knew in high school—there was one in every high school—who made his own chain mail. They were both pale and rigidly hunch-shouldered, even as young men, as though they had constantly to guard the small territory they had been allotted in life.

Did you notice how in the letter she keeps referring to me as "the bear"? I said. No wonder she didn't know I was a girl, she doesn't even know I'm *human*! And incidentally, I added, when the manager said nothing, you would think she'd be more understanding of the requirements of my position—we are, after all, both performers.

The manager seemed offended that I would compare myself, a sweating, hulking bear, to a clean, famously fresh-faced girl, our local celebrity, and I was let go. This wasn't dinner theater, he said, and at headquarters, where he sent me, I was told I could continue to be a polar bear but not solo or in a contact setting. This meant I could work corporate shows, which in our area never occurred. I saw myself telling my story on "People's Court," on "Hard Copy," but I was a big, unphotogenic girl and I knew people would not feel sympathy for me. Plus, in the few years since college I had been fired from every job I'd had, for actual transgressions—rifling aimlessly through a boss's desk drawers when she was out of the office; sweeping piles of hair into the space behind the refrigerator in the back room of a salon; stopping in my school bus, after dropping off the last of the children, for a cold Mr. Pibb at Suwannee Swifty—and I believed absolutely in retribution, the accrual of cosmic debt, the granting and revoking of amnesty. I was, simply, no longer innocent. I was not innocent, even as I protested my innocence.

No, I hadn't molested the girl, but even as I'd sat in the manager's office I could still smell the clean spice of her perfume, feel the light weight of her hands on either side of my head, a steady, intoxicating pressure even through plaster and fake fur. I could not fully believe myself, sitting there, to be an outraged, overeducated young woman in a bear suit. Beneath the heavy costume, I was the beast the manager suspected me of being, I was the bear.

The girl had been shopping with her mother, a bell-shaped generic older woman in a long lavender raincoat. The moment they rolled their cart around the corner into my aisle, still forty feet away, the model screamed. She was only eighteen, but still I was surprised—I would have thought Florida natives would be accustomed to seeing large animals in everyday life. She screamed: Oh my god, he's so cute! She ran for me, and I made some ambiguous bear gesture of acknowledgment and surprise. Hey there, sweetie, she said, pursing her lips and talking up into my face as though I were her pet kitten. I scooped a cone of chocolate chip for her but she didn't even notice. Mom, look, she yelled.

The lavender-coated mother approached without hurry or grace. Her face, up close, was like the Buddha's, and she took the ice cream from my paw automatically, as though we had an understanding. The model was rubbing my bicep with both of her narrow tanned hands. He's so soft, she said. I faced her, making large simpering movements, and noticed the small dark shapes of her nipples, visible through her white lacy bodysuit. I blushed, then remembered I needn't blush, and that was when she reached for me, pulling my hot, oversized head down to her perfect, heart-shaped face. The kiss lasted only a moment, but in that moment I could feel how much she loved me, feel it surging through my large and powerful limbs. *I am the bear*, I thought. Then it was over, and I remembered to make the silly gestures of a human in a bear suit pretending to be embarrassed. The model's mother had produced a small, expensive-looking camera from some hidden pocket of her raincoat and matter-of-factly snapped a photo of me, a bear pretending to be a friendly human, with my arm around the model's skinny shoulders, my paw entangled in her silky, stick-straight golden hair.

They left then, the mother never speaking a word, and they were all the way down the aisle, almost to the other end, when the produce manager stuck his head around the corner right in front of them and yelled my name, I had a phone call. The model looked back once before they disappeared, and though she never saw my face—I wasn't allowed to take off my head in public—it was obvious from her expression that she understood. It was an expression of disturbed concern, the way she might look if she were trying to remember someone's name or the words to a song she once knew well, but there was something else, too, a kind of abashed sadness that looked out of place on her young, milky face.

• • •

I could imagine how she must have felt, having once fallen in love with an animal myself in the same swift, irrevocable way I imagined she had. *The Good-Night Horse*, he'd been called—that heading had appeared beside his picture on the wallpaper in our cottage's bathroom at the Sleepy Hollow resort, and the words stayed in my head for years, like a prayer. The wallpaper featured reprints of antique circus posters and flyers, the same six or seven over and over, but the Good-Night Horse was the only one

I paid attention to: he was a powerful black shape that seemed to move and change form like a pile of iron shavings under a magnet, quivering slightly. He was muscular, a stallion. I was six. "Katie is masturbating," my mother said, in her mock-weary, matter-of-fact voice.

I would lie on the floor on my side under the toilet-paper dispenser, my face a few inches from the wall. The Good-Night Horse was shown in a series of four different postures. In the first two pictures he was wearing boots and trousers on his hind legs, but in the wild third picture, my favorite, he was tearing the trousers off dramatically. Clothes were flung on the ground all around him, his tail swished in the air, and the trousers waved wildly from his mouth. In the last picture he was, with his teeth, pulling back the covers of a single bed with a headboard, like my bed at home. "The World's Greatest Triumph of Animal Training," the poster said.

There was no problem with my masturbating, because my parents were agnostic intellectuals; they had given me a booklet called "A Doctor Talks to Five- to Eight-Year-Olds" that included, as an example of the male genitalia, a photograph of Michelangelo's statue of David. The photo was small and black-and-white, so you couldn't really get a good look at what was between his legs, but it appeared lumpy and strange, like mashed potatoes, and I found it unsettling. The book had already given me a clear picture of sexual intercourse: it was a complicated, vaguely medical procedure in which you were hooked up to an adult man and microscopic transactions then occurred. And though my parents had said, "You're probably too young to picture it, but someday you'll understand," I *could* picture it—I saw an aerial view of me, naked, and the statue of David lying side by side on a white-sheeted operating table, me in braids and of course only half his height. But this vision was the furthest thing from my mind when I looked at the Good-Night Horse.

I wasn't stupid, I knew people didn't marry horses, or any other animal. I just wasn't convinced that the Good-Night Horse was necessarily an animal—the more I looked at his picture, the more he seemed to be a man in some important sense. It was not his clothes, or the tricks he did, but something both more mysterious and more obvious than that. He reminded me a little of Batman—and, like Batman, he might have a way of getting out of certain things, I thought. He was sensitive, certainly—his forelock hung boyishly, appealingly, over his eyes, and his ears stood up straight, pointing forward in a receptive manner (except in the trouser-flinging picture, where they lay flat back against his head)—but you could tell that he was in no way vulnerable, at least not to the schemes and assaults of ordinary men. He was actually *more* a man than ordinary men, and something began to swell in my chest unbearably after a few days, weighing me down so that I could not possibly get off the floor, and my father finally had to carry me, sobbing, from the bathroom. I was sobbing not only because the Good-Night Horse and I could never meet, but because I understood with terrible certainty, terrible finality, that I would never be happy with anything less.

And it was true that no man had yet lived up. I had been engaged once to a social theorist who was my age but refused to own a TV and said things like "perused" in regular conversation and expected what he called my "joyous nature" to liberate him, but it ended when I discovered while he was writing his thesis that he had not gotten around to treating his three cats for tapeworm and had been living with them—the cats and the worms—contentedly for weeks. And now, at twenty-eight, I only dated, each man seeming a degree more aberrant than the last. The last had been a stockbroker who was hyperactive (rare in adults, he said) and deaf in one ear—he yelled and slurred and spit when he talked and shot grackles with an AK-47 from his apartment window, but was wildly energetic even late at night, boyish and exuberant and dangerous all at once, a little like the horse. On our second and last date, however, he took me to an Irish pub to meet his old college roommate, and the roommate engaged me in an exchange of stomach-punching to show off how tightly he could clench his abs, only when it was his turn to punch mine he grabbed my breasts instead, causing the stockbroker to go crazy. He dragged the roommate out onto the sidewalk and pushed him around like a piece of furniture he could not find the right place for, and I kept yelling that it was only a joke, I didn't mind, but in the scuffle the stockbroker's visor—the kind with the flashing colored lights going across the forehead band—got torn off and flung into the gutter, its battery ripped out, and when the fight was over he sat on the curb trying in vain to get it to light up again and saying, "He broke my fucking visor, man," until I told him I was taking a cab home, at which point he spit, on purpose, in my face.

So I could understand how the model might feel. I could see how, from looking at me, the miserable, small-minded Winn-Dixie manager would believe I had no business comparing myself to her, but, not being a bear himself, he did not understand that appearances meant nothing. I was a beast, yes, but I also had something like x-ray vision; I was able, as a bear, to see through beauty and ugliness to the true, desperate and disillusioned hearts of all men.

• • •

It was not difficult to figure out where she lived. She had been profiled earlier that month on "Entertainment Tonight" along with her sister, who at twelve was also a model, and the two girls were shown rollerblading around their cul-de-sac, and I knew all the cul-de-sacs in town from having driven the bus. So, a few days after I was fired, I drove to the house. To be a bear was to be impulsive.

It had been a record-hot, record-dry July, and the joke topic of the radio call-in show I listened to as I drove was "What have we done to antagonize God?" Callers were citing recent sad and farcical events from around the world in excited, tentative voices, as though the jovial DJ would really give them the answer, or as though they might win something. Only a few callers took the question personally, confessing small acts of betrayal and deception, but the DJ cut these people off. "Well, heh heh, we all do the best we can," he said, fading their voices out so it would not sound as though he were hanging up on them in mid-sentence. *Asshole*, I thought, and I made a mental note to stop at the radio station sometime and do something about him.

The model's house was made of a special, straw-colored kind of brick, rare in the South, or so "ET" had said. I saw the model's mother step out onto the front steps, holding a canister of Love My Carpet, but when she saw my car she stepped quickly back inside. The model's sister answered the door. She was a double of the model, only reduced in size by a third and missing the model's poignance. Her face was beautiful but entirely devoid of expression or history; her small smooth features did not look capable of being shaped by loss or longing, not even the honest longing of children. This would be an asset for a model, I imagined, and I could see where the mother's Buddha-nature had been translated, in her younger daughter, into perfection: desire had not just been eliminated, but seemed never to have existed in the first place.

"I am a fan," I said, and, perhaps because I was a girl, showered and combed and smiling, I was let in. I had also brought, as props, a couple of magazines which I held in front of me like a shield, but I was not nervous at all. I understood that I had nothing to lose, that none of us, in fact, had as much to lose as we believed. I sensed other bears out there, too—my fierce brothers, stalking through woods and villages, streams and lots, sometimes upright and sometimes on all fours, looking straight ahead and feeling the world pass beneath their heavy, sensitive paws.

The model's sister led me past ascending carpeted stairs and a wall of framed photos to the back of the house, where the model's bright bedroom overlooked a patio crowded by palmetto and bougainvillea, visible through sliding glass doors. A tiny motion sensor stuck to the wall above the glass blinked its red light as I entered. The model was bent over her single bed, taking small towels of all colors and patterns from a laundry basket, folding them, and placing them in piles. "Fan," the little sister said, and the model straightened and smiled and came forward, her perfume surrounding me and sending a surge of bear power through me, a boiling sheet of red up before my eyes. For just a moment as we shook hands I was sure she would know, she would remember the feel of my paw. But then she stepped back and my face cooled.

"I'm a huge fan," I said.

"Well thanks, that's so sweet," she said. She had taken the magazines from me automatically, just as her mother had taken the ice cream at the store, and was already scribbling across the shiny likeness of her face. "Should I make it out to anyone?" she said.

"My boyfriend," I said, and I told her the stockbroker's name.

"You're so lucky you're so tall," she said, handing the magazines back. "That's my biggest liability, I can't do runway. Well, thanks for coming by."

I looked around at the white dressers, the mirrored vanity, not ready to leave, and was shocked by a short row of stuffed bears set up on a shelf on the wall behind me. They were just regular brown teddy bears with ribbon bows at their necks, no pandas or polar bears, but they stared back at me with identical shocked expressions, another motion sensor glowing on the wall over their heads, unblinking. "Nice bears," I finally said, forcing myself to turn away.

"Oh, I've had those forever," she said. "See that one in the middle, that looks so sad? I found him in the street when I was six years old! Doesn't he look sad?"

"Yeah, he really does," I said. The bear was smaller and more lumpish than the other bears, with black felt crescents glued on for eyebrows.

"I used to make them take turns sleeping in the bed with me," the model said. "But even if it wasn't his turn I let him, just 'cause he looked so sad. Isn't that funny? I used to kiss him thirty-two times every night, right after I said my prayers."

"Thirty-two," I said.

"My lucky number," she said brightly.

"But you don't kiss him anymore," I said.

She stared at me, frowning. "No," she said. She stared at me some more and I just stood, my arms hanging, as a bear would stand, waiting. "Well, I better get back to work," she said.

"On your towels," I said.

She put her hands on her hips and gazed helplessly at the towels, as though they had betrayed her. "They're dish towels, isn't that queer?" she said. "I got them from a chain letter. My cousin started it, and I was second on the list, so I got, like, seventy-two of them sent from, like, everywhere. Isn't that pathetic—she's, like, twenty, and that's her *hobby*. You can have one, you want one?"

"Seriously?" I said.

"God, take your pick," she said. "I guess I have to remind myself sometimes that not everyone's as lucky as me, but, like, dish towels, I'm sorry."

I had to brush past her to get to the bed, the snap on the hip pocket of my jeans rubbing her arm. I took the top towel from the nearest stack, a simple white terrycloth one with an appliqué of a pair of orange and yellow squash. "Thanks, I'll think of you every time I use it," I said. I held the towel, stroking it. It was not enough, I was thinking.

"Well, thanks for coming by," she said. She had moved to the doorway and stood looking at me in the same way she had looked at the towels. The row of bears watched from over her shoulder, the slumped, sad one seeming braced by its brethren. I imagined the model and her soulless sister laughing at me after I'd gone, at my terrible size, my obvious lie about a boyfriend.

"I really have to get back to what I was doing . . ." she said.

"I'm sorry, I was just so nervous about finally meeting you," I said, and I could see her relax slightly. "I almost forgot to ask, isn't that funny? I hate to ask, but do you by any chance give out photos?"

"No, you'd have to contact the fan club for that," she said. Her face was final, and I turned, finally, to go. "But actually, wait," she said. "I do have something, if you want it."

What happened next was certainly not believable in the real world, but in the just, super-real world of the bear it only confirmed what I had known. She slid an envelope out from beneath the blotter on her white desk, picked through it with her slim graceful fingers, and pulled out a photograph which she passed to me hurriedly, as though it were contaminated. "Here, isn't that cute?" she said, laughing in a forced way, like the DJ.

There we were, her and me, her small, radiant face beside my large, furry, inscrutable one, my paw visible, squeezing her small shoulders together slightly, the flash reflected in the freezer cases behind us, making a white halo around both of our heads. Something seemed to pop then, noiselessly, as though the flash had just gone off around us again in the bedroom. Like a witch or spirit who could be destroyed by having her photo taken, I felt I was no longer the bear. "He's so cute," I murmured.

She snorted, but it had no heart to it, it sounded like she was imitating someone. Then for a moment she no longer saw me; she just stood there looking at nothing, her dark blue eyes narrowed, the faintest suggestion of creases visible around her mouth.

I had to take a step back, such was the power of her face at that moment. Then she too became herself again, and we were just two sad girls standing there, one of them beautiful and one of them something else. "Well, goodbye," I said, and she looked relieved that I was leaving—but also, I thought, that it was only me deserting her and not, as before, the heartbreaking, duplicitous bear.

On the way out I encountered her mother, who had materialized again beside the front door. It was the simple gravity, the solid, matter-of-fact weight of the woman, I decided, that made her silent appearances and disappearances so disconcerting, so breathtaking. Wasn't it more impressive to see a magician produce from the depths of his bag a large, floppy rabbit, to see the ungraceful weight of the animal dragged up into the light, than to watch him release doves or canaries, already creatures of the air, flashy but in their element? "Goodbye," I said. "Sorry."

She smiled and did not step but rather shifted several inches so that I could get past her, and then stood in the open doorway, round and lavender, smiling and watching my retreat. Only when I was halfway down the walk to my car did she say good-bye, and then her voice was so deep and strange and serene that I was not sure if I had really heard it or, if I had, if it had really come from her.

• • •

I did use the towel and sometimes think of the model when I used it. The photo I didn't frame or hide or treat with any cere-mony, but I did look at it often, trying to experience again that moment of transformation, that rush of power that had gone through me in the seconds before it was snapped.

But after a few months even the memory of it became weak. I was after all no longer the bear and could no longer remember well what it felt like to be the bear. The animal in the picture ap-peared only to be a big, awkwardly constructed sham, nothing you could call human. When I looked at it I felt only confusion and shame. How had I become that shaggy, oversized, hollow thing? Once I had been an honest little girl, a girl who had to be dragged away from the object of her love, but somehow, some-where, everything had changed. How had it happened? I won-dered. I studied the photo as though the bear could answer me, but it only stared back with its black fiberglass eyes, its grip on the real human beside it relentless.

The Flannery O' Connor Award for Short Fiction

. . .